PSYCHO B*TCHES

RICK WOOD

ALSO BY RICK WOOD

The Sensitives:

Book One – The Sensitives

Book Two – My Exorcism Killed Me

Book Three – Close to Death

Book Four – Demon's Daughter

Book Five – Questions for the Devil

Book Six - Repent

Book Seven - The Resurgence

Book Eight - Until the End

Shutter House

Shutter House

Prequel Book One - This Book is Full of Bodies

Cia Rose:

Book One – After the Devil Has Won

Book Two – After the End Has Begun

Book Three - After the Living Have Lost

Chronicles of the Infected

Book One – Zombie Attack

Book Two – Zombie Defence

Book Three – Zombie World

Standalones:

When Liberty Dies

I Do Not Belong
Death of the Honeymoon

Blood Splatter Books
Psycho B*tches
Home Invasion

Anthologies
Roses Are Red So Is Your Blood
Twelve Days of Christmas Horror
Twelve Days of Christmas Horror Volume 2

Sean Mallon:
Book One – The Art of Murder
Book Two – Redemption of the Hopeless

The Edward King Series:
Book One – I Have the Sight
Book Two – Descendant of Hell
Book Three – An Exorcist Possessed
Book Four – Blood of Hope
Book Five – The World Ends Tonight

Non-Fiction
How to Write an Awesome Novel

Thrillers published as Ed Grace:

The Jay Sullivan Thriller Series
Assassin Down
Kill Them Quickly

For Lizzy,

EXCERPT FROM WHEN WOMEN ATTACKED PODCAST EPISODE 1 (TRANSCRIPT)

I'm not quite sure where to start with this, to be honest with you.

I know what you mean.

It's like, this was so unexpected. So bizarre. And it's still so surreal, however much we've adjusted to what life is like now.

I'm not sure we can ever fully adjust to how life is now.

I mean, women were supposed to be maternal. Kind. The ones who kept us in check.

I'd go one step further than that – most murders are committed by men. *Were*, I mean. And very much so. Wives were far, far more likely to be killed by husbands. It was female prostitutes who were in danger. It was women who were made to feel unsafe by the comments of men who walk past them in the street. A short skirt seemed like a good enough excuse for a man to strip a woman of her dignity.

So this begs the question, then... what happened?

Ah, well. I think we all know the story by now.

We do, yes. Anyone who is listening will have some horrific stories to tell.

I don't think there isn't someone listening who hasn't lost a loved one, or hasn't been attacked by loved ones. And the change in women seemed so sudden – but, if we're honest, we'd been noticing a difference for some time.

And your role, if I'm right, is to record all of this.

Yes, that is correct. I wrote history books before this happened, and I have been asked to record the events for future generations – should we find a way to have any future generations, that is – to understand what happened.

And how are you finding it?

Well, a little tricky. See, there is something quite unique about recording recent events.

What's that?

History is written by those who win. All throughout time, the history books are written by the victors. This may be, in fact, the first time that history is written by the losers.

So it's going to be a very different account, then.

Not necessarily. Even though it's written by those who lost, it still has a very strong similarity to the history books by those who won.

How's that?

It is still written by men.

(*Laughs.*) Well that's certainly true.

But I believe that if we are to understand what actually happened, we have to separate ourselves from our gender. We can't afford to be biased in the way the male patriarchy always has.

I don't follow.

We need to understand why this happened. And we can't do that when the events of history have been recorded from our very limited perspective. Men will only be able to look at the situation from the point of view that women are evil.

What's the alternative? That we sympathise with them?

I think it's something to consider.

(*Scoffs.*) Why would you want to sympathise with such monstrous, barbaric, evil creatures?

(*Chuckles.*) The way you asked that question, my friend, outlines the exact reason why. You have already answered your own point.

I don't understand.

Then think about it. Hopefully, at some point, maybe when you're drifting off to sleep, it will click. And you will know.

Know what?

(Silence.)

Know what?

(Silence.)

What?

CHAPTER ONE

THERE HAS BEEN a lot of debate about whether twin intuition is real. Scientists have argued about whether there is some possible psychic intuition between twins, or whether this is absolute nonsense.

Of course, in a modern era such as ours, you would imagine scientists would reject any suggestions of psychic phenomena. Yet, I can tell you with no doubt whatsoever, that twin intuition is far from nonsense – in fact, it is the truest thing I've ever heard.

Me and Kaylee had it since the day we were born, nineteen years and sixty-eight days ago, when she appeared first and I followed ten minutes later – which sums us up, really; she arrives on time, and I'm always the straggler who arrives late. She would always meet all of life's turning points shortly before I did – when she learned to walk, when she drew her first picture, said her first word; it would always be just before I did.

I didn't mind, really. A lot of brothers might find this kind of thing annoying, but I never did. I found it endearing.

Don't get me wrong, we aren't the kind of twins that

merge into the same person; we still have our own personalities. But we have always had a connection no one can touch, and any similarities that occur in both of us are not annoying mimicry, but evidence of our impenetrable connection.

The main way we're different, really, is that she can walk into a room like she owns it, whereas I walk into a room and stand wherever I'm unnoticed. That's why I am how I am – if she walks into a room so boldly, it's quite easy to hide behind her.

I also heard someone say that, apparently, forty percent of twins invent their own language. This is true, though I refute the notion that the language was invented – we never deliberately sat down and planned out what word meant what; the language was just there. Often, it was spoken without words. A look or a glance could be enough to let the other know we are feeling sad, or happy, or even hungry.

In nineteen years, we have barely spent a day apart, never mind months. Which is why I was so devastated when, six months ago, Kaylee announced she was leaving to go to university.

I shouldn't really be mad, I get that. We aren't kids anymore. We need to decide what to do with our own lives. I mean, we took a gap year out to spend more time together, not wanting to let go of the bond we have, and we both even worked at the same bookstore.

But when January came around and I applied for the management scheme, she'd already applied to UCAS.

She's going to study English Literature of all things. I mean, we work in a bookstore. Is that not as close to literature as one can get?

The worst part? She's going to Edinburgh University. Not that I dislike Edinburgh, it's a lovely place – but I live in Cheltenham. That is more than a five-hour drive to Edinburgh. Not something that's easy to do on a whim.

If I'm honest, my negative reaction isn't just because I will miss her, or that I care about her, or want her near – although I feel all those things. It's that I've never been able to stick up for myself without Kaylee around. If someone ever said something nasty to me at school, she would kick them in the knee cap. If I was nervous about having to give a presentation in class, she would talk to me beforehand and calm me down. Even now, as adults, I will be in a social situation and panic for absolutely no reason, just feeling overwhelmed by the amount of people in the room, and she is the one who can see this in my face, and she knows exactly what to say to ground me.

How the hell am I supposed to break out of my timid shell without her there to smash it for me?

"Can I have everyone's attention?" my boss says. It is an hour after closing and we've all stuck around for a goodbye and congratulations on her last day at the store, and the last day before she leaves. "Kaylee, congratulations on your university place, but I have to ask – how are we ever going to replace you? We do not want you to leave but, in your absence, I guess Kevin will have to do!"

A few polite titters and chuckles respond, and people glance in my direction. Only Kaylee can tell that my smile isn't real.

"In all seriousness, it has been lovely to have you work here, the customers have adored you, and we are going to be sad to see you go."

The other six people who work here clap. Everyone looks at Kaylee, expecting her to say a few words. She shoots me her *help me* look, but I know she doesn't mean it. She's never had trouble capturing an audience.

"Thank you for your kind words," she says. "I can't believe it's been over a year since Kevin and I walked through those doors, two little dorks hoping for a job. I guess the only thing that's changed is you just have one little dork now."

More titters, more chuckles, more glances at me. I wish I could crawl into a hole where they wouldn't be able to look at me.

"Honestly, I have really enjoyed being amongst books all day, and I will miss you all. So thank you. Really."

More clapping.

"And I promise I will try and buy as many of my textbooks from you as I can."

More laughs, and Kaylee stands down from her place at the front, greeted with hugs and handshakes.

The boss fills up a few flutes with Prosecco. I take mine and meander past the stairs, sitting on a chair by the biography section. The face of some smug footballer grins at me on the cover of a book, and I respond with my middle finger.

I drop my head against the back of the chair, close my eyes, and think back to when we were kids. Our older sister, Shania, would always be wearing lipstick and going out with boys and causing issues for our parents. We'd be sat there, happily playing, my Action Men taking her Barbies for a ride in the jeep.

Those Action Men and Barbies are still in the attic somewhere, I imagine. Not that Mum or Dad would take me seriously if I asked for them to bring them down. We're probably too old for that now.

"You're fiddling with your lip again," comes a familiar voice.

"I'm allowed to."

"But I keep telling you; it makes you look like a knobhead."

"Well, there's another one of our similarities."

I open my eyes. She's grinning at me. I smile back.

"When are you going to stop sulking and come join the party?" she asks.

"Party? We're half the ages of most of the people here."

"They are nice people."

"Very nice. Almost nice enough to make you stay."

"Oh, come on, Kevin. We knew this day was going to come. We can't live together in mum and dad's house forever. At some point we are going to have to grow up."

I stand.

"And is that what you're doing, growing up?"

She chuckles at the insult. She always does that. I try and tease her or be mean, and she just finds it funny.

She places her thumbs either side of my mouth and spreads them across my cheeks, forcing a smile that is in no way genuine.

"There," she declares. "Doesn't look so bad."

I take her hands away. Look down.

"I will miss you too, you know," she tells me.

"Yeah…"

"It's just like Hannah said when she went off to uni and dumped you. You can't expect us to stay in school for the rest of our lives, can you?"

"Thanks for bringing that up."

"You're welcome."

She puts her arm around me and uses it to pull me through the bookstore to where everyone else is gathered.

I know I'm being immature. I get it. It's just tough, you know?

I'm not just letting go of Kaylee, I'm letting go of my childhood.

Now I have to enter the world of adulthood. Start my management training at this bookstore. Pay my parents rent, make my own meals; hell, maybe even get a mortgage and get married.

Married?

Mortgage?

Bleurgh. Can you imagine anything worse?

I sigh.

I am all alone, my best friend is leaving, and I can't imagine anyone having a worse day than me.

Little do I know, a man in Yorkshire is about to have his bollocks bitten off.

CHAPTER TWO

CHET IS as arrogant as he is guilty.

Of course he didn't have consent. Of course the girl was too drunk. Of course a guy like him didn't give a shit about the feelings of some slut.

But that's the great thing about the legal system in this country – his past treatment of the opposite sex was not allowed to be brought into the trial, yet *hers* was. As soon as the jury found out what a little slag she was, her prosecution was as good as done.

Why would his history of consistently being accused by drunk women of inappropriate behaviour matter? Why would his lecherous treatment of women in the office be relevant? Why on earth would they need to know how many women he kissed on a night out, when they could hear about a woman who gets wasted and sleeps with a different man every weekend?

In the end, she could not be trusted as a reliable witness, and Chet was able to walk out of that courthouse, a free man.

And now he stands in his garage with his tools, tinkering with the engine of his BMW while his wife, who is stupid enough to believe he was innocent, sits inside with their obese child.

His BMW hadn't been purring like it usually did, but after some twisting and turning of a few cogs he'd have his pussy magnet ready soon.

Outside the open garage door, the rain is getting heavier. Puddles expand on the drive, and pellets of rain thud from the sky like the devil's angry piss.

"Fuck a duck," he says, gazing into the dim evening sky, raising an eyebrow at the violence of the rain being thrown in every direction by the furious wind. After giving the weather a moment's attention, he turns back to the engine and continues tinkering.

Something, however, catches his eye, and he turns back, staring intently into the storm.

Across the drive is a figure. A person. A woman, in fact. A silhouette. One that seems very familiar.

He can't make out any of her facial features, as the torrential rain is obscuring the space between the garage and the end of the drive, but the outline of the black figure hovers, hunched over, arms dangling like a demented puppet, her fingers curled like claws. She's panting, her whole body heaving up and down with her heavy breaths.

He recognises her; he's sure he does.

Hang on, is that…

No, it can't be.

He squints, trying to make out a face, or the tattoo on her arm, or any other distinguishing feature. He edges to the garage doorway, pausing just before the water hits him, peering through the darkness of the downpour.

"Hello?" he shouts.

Nothing. The figure remains hunched, panting, not moving.

"Oi, you fucking want something or what?"

Still no reply.

He steps forward slightly, allowing a few trickles of rain to hit the bottom of his grey tracksuit and his Adidas trainers.

"Who the fuck are–"

Her head lifts.

"Oh, Jesus, you got to be fucking kidding me!"

There is no doubt. It is her. His accuser. Standing at the end of his drive like some demented rabid beast. Probably drunk. Or high.

"You don't get it, love – you lost! Give it up, darling."

A long and slimy tongue edges out of her mouth and licks her lips. Thick drool oozes out. He is sure he can see blood trickling down her chin, but the rain washes it away too quickly to tell.

"Oi, piss off!"

He considers threatening to call the police, but they have never had his back. No, he will deal with this himself.

He picks up the spanner and holds it high.

"See this? You're on my property. I can legally beat the shit out of you. So back the fuck off, yeah?"

She does not back away. In fact, this foolish hussy actually begins to hobble forward.

And the word is *hobble,* not *walk* – there is something inhuman about the way she moves. She is limping, shuffling slightly, edging with each bone moving in a different direction.

"Holy shit," Chet says. "What the fuck has happened to you?"

He doesn't know whether he should be curious, sympathetic, or scared.

He shakes his head defiantly and scratches *scared* off the list straight away – no bitch is going to make him scared.

She keeps shuffling, dragging her feet until she's halfway

across the drive, her mouth opening and closing like she's trying to chew something that isn't there.

"Alright, that's enough, you can stop there."

She doesn't stop.

"Oi, you fucking listening to me or what?"

She stretches her arms out, her fingers with their filthy fingernails reaching for him.

"You lost the trial, it's done, it's over, now back off!"

She approaches, until she's almost in touching distance, and as she comes further into the light of the single orange bulb above the BMW, her battered flesh becomes visible. Her eyes are fully dilated, her bruised skin sagging, her greasy hair matted with dried blood.

"I said fuck off!"

He wouldn't admit it, not to himself or anyone else, but a tinge of fear burns into his chest. A queasiness rises through him as he stares at her dishevelled appearance; so different to the tidy, well-groomed, well-dressed woman in court. What exactly is she planning to do once she reaches him?

Her fingers reach out and brush his chin, leaving a greasy mark over his stubble. He grabs his spanner and uses it to threaten her.

"I mean it – fuck off!"

She is not deterred and, as her chattering teeth almost reach his throat, he lifts the spanner high and brings it down upon her head.

She collapses at his feet, still, and Chet is at first concerned, then annoyed – he hopes he doesn't have to go through another trial for this.

What if he just killed her? Disposed of the body? But then what? He doesn't want to get her blood over his car.

He puts his hands on his hips. Contemplates what to do. Which is a mistake, as he doesn't notice her lifting her head and eyeing up his crotch.

As he considers how big the boot of his BMW is, and whether he has anything he can put her in so he doesn't stain the upholstery, she leaps up with speed far more rapid than the slow, stoic movements she had approached with, and clamps her teeth around his scrotum.

He screams. Oh boy, does he scream. Like a fucking pansy.

But even his wife doesn't come out to check if he's okay. She assumes he's being a prick, doing some practical joke where he'll film her reaction and put it on YouTube, like he's done before – he has a whole load of viral videos where he torments her, and he has evidently cried wolf enough times for her to ignore his shouts.

He strikes the spanner against her head again, which knocks her back, but does not loosen her grip; meaning that, as she falls to the floor, she takes his testicles with her.

Chet can do nothing but cry, bleed, and watch as her mouth devours his most precious assets. She chews like she's working her way through a well done steak, savouring every taste, letting the juices run down her chin, staring back at him as she swallows with a satisfaction that only follows the most succulent of meals.

He turns to run, limping away through the rain, weeping desperately, but the searing pain between his thighs stops him from being able to move quickly. She pursues him, but she is not hobbling forward anymore; she is sprinting like he's never seen someone sprint before. It takes seconds for her to catch up with him, dive upon his back, and take him to the floor.

She sinks her teeth into his throat, digs in, hard, then harder still, until her teeth penetrate his windpipe. She pulls her teeth away, skin and blood wedged in the cracks of her teeth, shaking her head, sending thick slabs of skin and meat flying against the brick wall of his family home.

She continues to devour his body long after he's dead. No neighbours can see through the storm, and those that can see a commotion think so little of Chet that they do not bother coming to help. In fact, they wonder if someone has finally brought the prick his comeuppance.

Well, my friends, someone has definitely brought him his comeuppance – there is no doubt about that.

CHAPTER THREE

It is tradition in my family that, when someone has a big life event, we have a meal to mark the occasion. When we turned eighteen, when my dad was given a promotion at work, when Shania graduated… Each of these were celebrated with one of my mum's roasts.

In fact, I'm fairly certain we've had at least six of these meals for Shania and at least five for Kaylee in the last year – whereas I struggle to think of one that we've had for me. But that's okay, I guess. Shania joined the police, while Kaylee was offered a university place and achieved a few rewards for some charity work she does – meanwhile, I work in a bookstore, with nothing else going on. Which is fine. They want something, they go for it – if I want something, I lay awake all night worrying about all the ways trying to achieve that thing could go wrong.

Today is an important meal, as Kaylee is going away, and although Mum declared this as her 'goodbye meal,' Kaylee insisted it was more of a 'see you later meal.' She gave me a quick look after she'd said it, as if to gauge my reaction; as if her statement was for my benefit.

So here we sit, sitting at the same places at the table that we sat when we weren't yet old enough to feed ourselves. Kaylee sits beside Shania, Mum is to my side, and Dad is at the head of the table. My parents are of the generation where Mum is expected to cook a large, lavish roast dinner, but Dad receives all the praise for carving the chicken. I always found it odd that Dad gets the applause despite Mum having spent three hours in the kitchen cooking – but, like most outdated traditions, we do it because that's just the way it's always been done.

"Is the car packed?" Mum asks Dad, once the chicken has been carved and we are all eating.

"Yep, just a few bags that Kaylee can take on the train, and we're done."

"Oh, you must be so excited," Mum directs at Kaylee.

She glances at me. Like she doesn't want to hurt my feelings by expressing how excited she actually is, like she needs my approval to say it; and I feel bad that she has to censor her enthusiasm on my behalf.

"Of course she is," I say reluctantly, still resenting the idea, but the smile on Kaylee's face shows that she's grateful.

"Just don't go shagging around in Fresher's Week like I did," Shania says, not lifting her face from her food. "Those bitches are full of crabs. And however fit they are when the beer goggles are on, they'll look like munters in the morning."

We all stop eating and stare at her. Not only is Shania a police officer who keeps the highest standards of respectability and political correctness, but SHAGGING is a word that none of us would ever dare say in front of our parents, just like words such as BITCHES, CRABS and MUNTERS.

I expect her to blurt out that she's making a really awful joke, but she doesn't; she is oblivious to our staring. Instead, she makes the moment even more uncomfortable by ditching her knife and fork and devouring her food with her mouth like a starving dog, pulling the skin off the chicken with her teeth and shovelling mushy peas into her mouth with her hands.

"Shania?" Mum says.

She doesn't hear.

"Shania?"

Too busy eating.

"Shania, I'm talking to you."

She shovels chicken and sprouts and carrots into her mouth – anything that can fit goes in.

"Shania!"

She finally notices and lifts her head, meat juice running down her chin and apple sauce smeared across her cheek.

"What?" she says, looking at each of us in turn.

"Is there something wrong with your knife and fork?"

She looks blankly at Mum, then to her cutlery.

"No, why?" she says.

Mum raises her eyebrows. Shania looks down at the meat on her hands and gravy running between her fingers.

"Oh," she realises, then picks up her knife and fork.

I go to look at Kaylee, hoping to exchange a look, but notice something out of the window behind her.

"What's that?" I say, peering out.

Everyone turns to look.

Our elderly next-door neighbour, Mrs Hogsmith, stands on the lawn.

"Do you think she's okay?" Kaylee asks.

"I'm not sure," Dad says. "She was diagnosed with dementia a few months ago, remember?"

"Well, where's Mr Hogsmith?" Mum interjects. "I thought he was taking care of her?"

"So did I. I'm sure he'll be out to collect her any moment."

We all watch and wait, but Mr Hogsmith does not come out. She just stands there, shifting her weight from one foot to the other, swaying side to side.

"She really doesn't look okay," I say. I excuse myself from the table and approach the window. She is wearing nothing but a night gown – the kind old women always seem to wear in movies; long and white, with old-fashioned lace at the base, revealing her thin, veiny legs as it wafts upwards in the breeze. Except, the night gown is not white anymore – there is a patch of red around the neckline, and around the crotch.

What is going on? I mean, I know she has dementia, but it doesn't make you bleed from random areas, does it? And it looks quite windy; surely she's cold?

She continues to sway from side to side, her head twitching violently, with her long, spindly arms randomly shifting in obscure directions. It's really disturbing and, honestly, freaks me out more than I'd admit aloud.

Still, I can't just leave her standing there, can I? I have to do something. She's an elderly neighbour who's ill, and I have to go help; it's the right thing to do.

I try not to feel freaked out as I head for the door, reminding myself she's just ill, that's all it is.

Just ill.

That's all...

"I'm going to go take her home," I announce as I put my shoes on and walk outside.

It's a cool evening, yet the closer I get to Mrs Hogsmith the more I see the beads of sweat trickling from her forehead, down her nose, her chin, and onto the dried blood of her gown; blood that seems to have crusted.

"Mrs Hogsmith, are you okay?"

She doesn't look up. She doesn't seem to react to me at all. She twitches a little, like there's a sudden jolt in her neck, and her arms abruptly move into another twisted position. It can't be comfortable to be standing in such a way.

I don't want to approach her. I don't want to go near her, she's scaring me. But that's what a child thinks, isn't it? *Oh no, can't approach, she's too freaky, she's a monster!*

But she's not a monster. She's just ill.

I wonder where Mr Hogsmith is. I go to knock on their front door and notice that it's open.

"Mr Hogsmith?" I call out.

Nothing.

Not a sound. Not even a movement.

Where could he be?

"Mr Hogsmith, are you there?"

Still nothing.

I sigh. Hesitate, then approach Mrs Hogsmith again, place one hand on her back, and use my other hand to take hold of her loose fingers. She stinks very strongly of piss, her bare feet are covered in mud, and her hair is soaked with grease.

Why has Mr Hogsmith let her get into this state?

"Come on, Mrs Hogsmith, let's get you home."

My fear subsides a little as we walk, slowly, shuffling forward, toward her front door.

We reach it and I help her step over the threshold to her home, guiding her inside.

"Mr Hogsmith?" I call out again.

Nothing.

"Just wait here," I tell her, leaving her by the kitchen door, and walking through the hallway, looking in rooms.

I see Mr Hogsmith's slippers in the living room, but no Mr Hogsmith. There is some random quiz show on the television, but no one watches it.

"What have you done with him?" I jest with Mrs Hogsmith – not that she'd comprehend the joke.

"Mr Hogsmith? Mr Hogsmith are you there?"

I see the back of a bench in the garden with two bare feet on the end of it. That's why he didn't hear me – he's asleep!

I can't quite see his face or his body, but I don't want to wake him. He's not moving at all, he must be quite asleep, so I return to where I left Mrs Hogsmith.

She is not there, however. She is now in the living room. With a fork in her hand. Jabbing it against her arm.

"Oh, Mrs Hogsmith, don't do that–"

I approach, but she twists around suddenly, and screeches at me – she actually screeches, like a banshee or a distressed bird or a pterodactyl from *Jurassic Park* or something.

She raises the fork in her hand. Her eyes are unnaturally wide, and they are focussed on me in a way I have never seen before.

"Screw this!"

I did what I needed to. I brought her in. I made sure she was okay. Now I really don't want her to hurt me.

"Mr Hogsmith, your wife needs help!" I call as loud as I can, so loud I must have woken him up. Still, I don't wait to see what she plans to do to me with that fork, so I run out of the house, closing the door behind me, and stride into the middle of the lawn.

I stare at their door, waiting for her to come out, panting more than I care to admit.

Nothing happens.

I wait. Preparing to run. To scream.

After a while, I realise I haven't moved, shaking with fear because of an ill woman in her nineties.

I shake my head to myself, and think about how much Kaylee would take the mickey, and how I cannot possibly tell my family what's actually happened.

"Is she okay?" Mum asks as I return home, bolt the door, and return to the dinner table.

"Yeah, fine."

"You gave her more attention than she deserves," grunts Shania. "That cunt was a filthy whore. Mr Hogsmith shouldn't have married such a slut."

We all look at Shania.

Perfect, polite, feminist Shania, speaking like she's possessed by someone she'd hate.

What the hell is going on?

EXCERPT FROM WHEN WOMEN ATTACKED PODCAST EPISODE 2 (TRANSCRIPT)

How long have you been a police officer?

I started as a PCSO when I was twenty-two, six months or so after uni. A year later I joined as a constable. I took the tests for Sergeant after two years, then inspector the next year – and I have stayed an inspector since.

How long's that?

Seven or eight years.

That's a long time.

It is.

And have you always been based in the MET?

I was originally stationed with the Shropshire constabulary, but moved to London when I met my wife, which is where I joined the MET. I've spent most of my career there.

EXCERPT FROM WHEN WOMEN ATTACKED PODCAST EPI...

I imagine the MET is slightly more-action packed.

(*Chuckles.*) Nowhere is an easy job, but I would say yes, the MET threw up more challenges.

Such as?

Oh, everything. Terrorists. I was there on London Bridge when the stabbings occurred, and it was my colleague that tackled the man before he could kill any more people. I have witnessed gun fights, something most officers don't experience in their careers. Discovered bodies. Fought drunks. I have seen it all, I suppose you could say.

And how does this compare to the events you're here to discuss?

(*Long pause.*) Yes, well, erm… I, er… I have witnessed awful things, I admit, of course, but never something quite so… surreal.

Surreal?

Yes. The reports began to come in about five in the morning, just as I was arriving to use the gym before my shift. Mostly of domestic violence, except, not like we're used to…

In what way?

It was rare we'd have a man reporting domestic abuse to us. It happened, but it was rare. That morning we had thirty-six calls, all from men.

Thirty-six?

That was just the first hour.

At what point did you start to twig that something was wrong?

By the second hour I knew. Just driving to these domestic disputes, you could see, something was changing. The women we drove past, they were… different.

More aggressive?

Yes, but not yet. They were walking more… Bolshy, I guess. With a swagger. Like they owned the place. It sounds ridiculous to say, but they were walking like men.

Like men?

Yes, except… I don't know. They weren't afraid to do so. Reporters seem to think that this whole thing just started, that women just randomly attacked their husbands and sons. But that wasn't the case. It was slow, subtle changes at first. Such as the way women walked.

But surely you're not just judging the change in women by the way they walked?

Everything about this was strange. And it wasn't just the walk. It was the way they chewed open mouthed, sat with their legs spread wide open, grinned at you like they were mentally undressing you and there was nothing you could do to stop them.

And how long did it take until the killing happened?

EXCERPT FROM WHEN WOMEN ATTACKED PODCAST EPI...

(Takes a moment to think.) I would say it happened within twenty-four hours.

And what happened then?

Chaos.

Did you at least fight back?

There were very few of us left to fight back. The female officers were attacking us and the number of male officers were quickly depleting. Within hours, they were in control.

Who was in control?

Them.

Who is *them*?

(Long pause.) The women.

CHAPTER FOUR

Kaylee and Dad are attempting to stuff all of her things into the car. It's quite a challenging task, considering Kaylee pretty much owns EVERYTHING. So much stuff, in fact, that she won't fit in the car with both Dad and her stuff, so is having to travel separately by train.

Honestly, she likes the film *Kill Bill* – which is an awesome movie, so of course she does – but that's not enough. Not only does she need to have it on DVD, she also needs to have it on Blu-Ray.

You'd think that's enough, right?

Nope. She imported the Japanese version on DVD as well because, or so she claims, there are some minute differences. A scene that is in black and white in our version is apparently in colour in the east. Honestly, I've never noticed a change myself, but Kaylee seems pretty adamant.

Then, a few months ago, they released a new cover for the Blu-Ray. Of course, that one was added to her collection. So now she has four copies of the same movie.

And that's just one movie – let's not even get started on all the other movies she intentionally has duplicates of.

So she is leaving for university, with all her variations of DVDs and books, as well as a television that is already too big for her generously sized room at home, along with numerous suitcases of clothes, many of which she hasn't worn. She's even packed her rounder's bat, adamant that she will join a rounder's society. She has been captain of *The Lightning Stars*, the leading team in Cheltenham's rounder's league; I've never had the heart to tell her it's just a game for children to play in PE classes.

I tried to help her pack, but Kaylee said I'd best leave it to them, and that I'd just get in the way. I wasn't sure whether to be offended or not, but if it means I can get out of lugging heavy boxes around, then hey, who am I to argue?

I leave them to it and wander into the living room, where I find Mum watching television.

"Oh, Kevin, come and watch this," she says, pulling me close, and I perch on the arm of her chair.

"What is it?" I ask, then notice how my mum is sitting. It's very… un-mum-like. Normally she'd be perched on the edge of the chair with her legs crossed, or sat back with a blanket on her lap. Right now, however, she is slouched down in her chair with her legs spread wide open, grandly displaying her crotch. Her fingers rest inside her trousers, just beneath the waistline, with a complete disregard for the discomfort placing your hands in such a position has for the rest of the people in the room.

"It's this wonderful woman, she's called Helen Field," Mum tells me, and I try to ignore her bizarre body language and focus on the television. "Honestly, this woman is so inspiring. The things she says, the empowering way she talks, the charity work she does. Look, they are showing an interview she did."

An outdated talk show host with a grey mullet and brown suit introduces Helen Field, and her husband Bill. Helen is a woman in her early thirties with long, blond hair and a wicked smile, wearing a perfectly fitted suit blazer and trousers. She is what my dad would refer to as a 'power woman.' Even I feel a little intimidated by her, and I'm only watching her on TV.

Her husband trails behind her in an ageing suit with his head down, clearly only there to fill a quota.

"Welcome, welcome!" the host says, shakes Helen's hand profusely, then gives Bill a kiss on the cheek. He directs them to their seats.

"Congratulations on the film, it must have been a great experience," the host says.

"It was, I played a small part as a speaker – not much acting there, really."

A few titters come from the audience.

"Oh, I'm sure there was," the host insists. "Tell me about it."

"Well, it was a brilliant opportunity to open up about problems facing our society on a bigger stage, and I really feel I managed to channel my energy into increasing the awareness. We live in a world where we teach our young to be quiet, when we should be teaching them to shout. We teach our old to stay in the background, when they should be teaching us about life. We keep our partners at home, when they should be sharing our experiences."

"Wonderful, just wonderful." The host turns to Bill. "And what do you plan on wearing to the film's premiere?"

This interview is weird. I'm not quite sure what it is, but it is making me feel uncomfortable.

I get up to go, but Mum grabs my arm and pulls me back, her grip leaving a mark on my skin.

"Wait, they are showing the Ted Talk she did, just watch."

The chat show cuts to Helen standing on a stage with TED in large red writing behind her.

"We live in a world where we can make a change, but we choose not to. Where we need to listen. Where we need to thrive."

"I'm just going to the toilet," I lie, and go to get up again.

Mum pulls me back again, holding onto my arm. She turns toward me and her face moulds into a look of disgust. I check to see if I have some of my breakfast on my face or something.

"What?" I ask. "What is it?"

"Is – is that what you're wearing?" she asks, looking me up and down.

I look down at my clothes. T-shirt and shorts. I don't understand what the problem is.

"Why?" I say. "What is it?"

"It's just, I don't know – it's a bit revealing, don't you think?"

"What?"

"I mean, you can see all of your legs."

Suddenly, I feel very uncomfortable. I didn't think there was anything wrong with wearing a pair of shorts. They aren't that short, are they? They go down to just above my knees.

"They don't seem that bad," I say.

"Yes, but when you sit down, you can see right up them."

"Can you?"

"I just think you're going to attract unwanted attention, don't you?"

"Unwanted attention?"

"Yes, you're just asking for it."

"Asking for what?"

"Just listen to your mother, please."

"I think they are fine, honestly."

I turn to go, but she grabs onto my arm again.

And my mother, who I have never heard swear in my life,

who barely had the ability to discipline us as a child, who always brought me and my friends trays of biscuits and drinks when they came over, who cried at the end of *Titanic*, who is the most caring, loving person I've ever known, turns to me, and says:

"Kevin – change the fucking shorts."

She says it with a smile, then turns back to Helen Field.

I rush out of the room.

CHAPTER FIVE

WITH THE CAR packed too full to fit Dad and Kaylee, I offer to walk with Kaylee to the train station, and we stroll in contented silence – with me now wearing trousers.

No silence between us has ever been uncomfortable – in fact, many meaningful moments happen when no one's talking. This is no exception.

We reach the station and look for the train on the departure screen. It is due to arrive on platform two in five minutes, and she has to cross the bridge to get to it.

I am not going to cross that bridge with her.

"I'll leave you here," I say.

"What's the matter?" she teases. "Don't want me to see your man-tears?"

I shrug. I look away. She's right, I don't.

As I try to distract myself, my gaze wanders to a bus stop where a woman sits, coughing repeatedly into a handkerchief. A man walks past and she wolf whistles at him, then continues to cough.

Hmm. How odd.

"You can come visit, you know," Kaylee says. "Any time you want."

"It's hardly a day's ride away."

"Then you can stay over. We'll top and tail it. Done it plenty of times before."

I look down.

"What is it, eh?" she asks. "You seem to think this is the end of us being twins or something. It's not. It's just… At some point, one of us was going to have to get a real job. Or buy a house. Or get married. What do you think will happen then?"

I shrug. She has a point, but I'd honestly never thought about it. I always imagined adulthood would be something that crept upon us slowly, and we'd have plenty of time to adjust, but I was wrong. Adulthood has arrived suddenly, kicked me in the balls, then laughed at my pain.

"This is really tough for me as well," she says. "This wasn't an easy decision. It's going to be the first time in our lives we are apart, and it sucks, but… That's growing up, I guess."

"I know. I just… wish we could be kids forever."

"We all do."

"I'm just not sure I even know how to stand up for myself or be brave without–"

A voice over the tannoy interrupts me to announce that her train will be arriving imminently.

We share another moment of silence.

"Well, that's me," she says.

"I guess it is."

She puts her arms around me, and I reciprocate. We give each other a long squeeze, like we did when we were kids and our parents tried to separate us, when Dad would try to take me for 'boy' activities and Mum would try and take her for 'girl' activities, and we'd refuse, saying we didn't want to do anything apart.

Then she breaks away, the hug is over, and she's leaving.

"See you later, dickhead," she says, glancing back at me with a smile.

"Later, Wolf," I say. I used to call her that for her obsession with Naomi Wolf's book *The Beauty Myth*. She read it at least ten times when we were teenagers.

She walks across the bridge, down the stairs, and disappears behind the train.

I turn away and pause, sighing. I force myself to lift my head up and I notice a woman, leant against her Ferrari, watching me, staring lecherously. It makes me feel really uncomfortable and I'm not sure what to say, so I pretend not to notice and walk on.

I leave the station, cross the road, and walk past a fish and chips shop, the smell of which makes me hungry. I wish I'd brought some cash with me.

A group of women outside the chippy are being rowdy and making a lot of noise, laughing and strutting around like they own the street. I catch a few snippets of conversation, things like "got to get that dick while it's fresh" or "he was a fucking munter" or "mate, it ain't rape if you shout surprise first."

I quicken my pace as I pass them, keeping my head down and hoping to remain unnoticed. I'm only halfway down the next street when a white van drives past, honking its horn, with a woman shouting something out of the window at me. I'm not quite sure what she says, but I definitely hear the words *strap-on* and *arsehole*.

I pull my jacket tightly around me, telling myself it's only a ten-minute walk home. I just feel so... unsafe.

I pass the supermarket, walk around the corner and cross over, next to the shop where Kaylee bought me the guitar I wanted for my fifteenth birthday, then onto the street where I threw up after drinking too much at seventeen and all my friends laughed – except for Kaylee, who made sure I was all right.

As I walk on, some shouting attracts my attention. It sounds aggressive. I stop, not quite sure where it's coming from, then realise it's from the window of a flat next to me.

Through the window, I see a woman standing over a man, screaming.

"Why are you going out dressed like a slut?" she demands, and I can see the spit raining over her boyfriend. "You're fucking asking for it! Whose attention are you after?"

"Please, I know this isn't you," the man says. "Stop being like this."

"Like what? What about that girl you were texting, what's she like? She fucking better than me?"

"We're just friends."

"I told you not to text her you fucking slag!"

I don't interfere. It's not my business. Just walk on. Ignore it, and walk on.

I keep walking until I reach home, and when I do, I open the door quickly and put the latch on, leaning against it, breathing heavily.

I mean, is it me, or does everything seem really weird today?

I walk past the kitchen, where Mum stands, and head for the stairs, where I pause. Did I just see what I think I saw?

I walk back to the kitchen, where Mum is standing, motionless, in front of the open fridge, staring.

"Mum?"

No answer.

"Mum, are you all right?"

Still nothing.

"Mum, what are you doing?"

I consider whether to approach her but, honestly, it's not

the strangest thing I've seen today, and I already feel pretty lousy – so I ignore it, and walk upstairs.

I pause outside Kaylee's room. Her bed is unmade, her bookcases are empty, and the walls are stripped of posters.

I shut her door and go to my room, close the curtains, put on some loud music, and stay there for the rest of the day.

CHAPTER SIX

IT'S the next day and Dad's doing this thing he often does on a Sunday, where he believes he's on *Gardener's World,* and thinks no one notices him narrating his actions under his breath as he scrambles around in the garden.

"And here you can see a troublesome plant that we are going to pick, let's see how best to deal with it shall we…" he says, not realising that he looks and sounds like a total nutter.

The only thing that makes this more ridiculous? The fact that he has no idea what he's doing. But, like anyone who's lived long enough to say *well that's how I've always done it and it's always been fine*, he refuses to listen to advice.

On today's episode, he is picking out weeds from the side of the lawn. Except, they are not weeds. There are thorny branches. And he is not wearing gloves. He wears gloves when he mows the lawn, but apparently not whilst picking thistles. Nevertheless, he determinedly ignores the pain and continues his narration with the occasional exclamative.

I watch him from the window, wondering what Kaylee is

doing and if she's made friends, or whether she went out last night to the fresher's party.

I hope she's happy. Really, I do. But it's odd that I haven't heard from her. I would have thought she'd have at least texted to let me know she's okay, or to check that I am. Either she's having too much fun or, like me, she is refusing to interrupt the other's life. Only difference is, my life is currently in a state of melancholy and could do with an interruption.

"And then we pull this weed and grab this one with your hand ow you son of a bitch and then we take this one with both hands ow you cock sucker and then we have the weed out!"

My thoughts stop as I notice something a few metres behind Dad's back – Mrs Hogsmith on our lawn again.

Only, she isn't staring absentmindedly. She is shifting her weight from one bare foot to the other like yesterday, only her eyes look less vacant, and more venomous. They are staring at Dad, who remains oblivious.

She wears the same night dress with the same splotches of blood; only the stains seem to have spread.

I knock on the window to try and alert Dad, but amongst the "now this is a stubborn weed we need to really pull out ah you piece of dog anus and it takes both hands to do so" he does not hear me.

This is getting slightly ridiculous. Where is Mr Hogsmith? He is meant to be her carer – so why isn't he coming to get her? How has she found her way out again?

I walk outside and go to approach Mrs Hogsmith, only I pause. Something's different. I feel more wary, though I'm not sure why, but as I scan the lawns of the adjacent houses, it becomes clearer.

Mrs Hogsmith is not the only woman outside her house, standing gormlessly. There are at least half a dozen more on our neighbour's lawns; some teenagers, some mothers, some children, all with blood either on their hands or on their clothes or, God knows why, around their mouth.

It is a bizarre sight, and one that makes my body turn rigid with fear. I decide to just get Mrs Hogsmith home, and get Dad back in the house – then we can figure out what's going on once we're safe.

Mrs Hogsmith edges closer to Dad, and her jaw starts snapping.

"Dad…"

Dad is still clueless.

"Dad, turn around…"

"I'm starting to think this would be better with gloves…"

"Dad!"

Finally, he turns to look at me.

"What?" he snaps.

"Look."

I lift my hand to indicate the random women on their lawns, all looking as equally disturbed as Mrs Hogsmith.

"What's going on?" He notices Mrs Hogsmith. "What are you doing out again, Mrs Hogsmith?"

He approaches her.

"Dad, don't," I say, though I don't know why. Mrs Hogsmith has always been perfectly nice, even in the midst of her dementia, which can cause some people to be aggressive.

"Why, Kevin? What is it?"

"I, just… I don't know. This doesn't feel right."

"Don't be preposterous. Mrs Hogsmith, are you okay?"

She smacks her lips together and lines of saliva spread from her top teeth to her bottom teeth. She dribbles, and it comes out in large gunks and expanding bubbles.

She will not stop staring at Dad's neck.

"Kevin, go get Mr Hogsmith."

Good idea. I rush to her house, where the door is already open, and peer in.

"Mr Hogsmith? Are you there?"

I search the kitchen, glance up the stairs, look in the living room where the television is on, but it is the garden where I find him. On the bench. In fact, he is in the exact same position he was in yesterday, and doesn't seem to have moved.

I mean, he could have chosen to spend his afternoon in the same place, but...

I approach him. Slowly. Cautiously. Listening carefully for any sudden noises.

"Mr Hogsmith?"

He doesn't answer.

A cat screeches to my right and it makes me jump. I don't notice at first, but the cat is dragging itself across the floor, a line of blood trailing behind it.

I hurry across the garden, and approach Mr Hogsmith again, quickly but warily.

As I approach the bench, I know. Somehow, I just know what I will find.

His mouth is wide open, as are his eyes. They stare up at the sky. His throat is slit. His trousers are down. His legs are covered in blood. The bench is covered in shit.

He stinks.

Like faeces and rotten eggs.

The blood is dry.

He hasn't just been killed.

Mr Hogsmith has been dead for days.

And Dad is outside with his killer.

CHAPTER SEVEN

I KNOCK over numerous tables and cups and plates as I battle my way out, emerging outside to see my Dad, having discarded his spade by the weeds, edging toward Mrs Hogsmith with his hand out.

"Dad, no!"

"Shush, Kevin," he says, in his *adults are talking now* voice.

"But Dad, she–"

"Kevin, please, you're not helping." He smiles widely at Mrs Hogsmith. "Mrs Hogsmith, please, you are not well, let me accompany you inside."

She growls.

She actually growls.

Not like a playful puppy growl – the kind of growl a lion unleashed from its cage would growl; assuming that the lion was demented, with rabies, and hell-bent on destruction.

"Dad, get away from her."

"Get away from her? She has dementia, Kevin, she's not a wild animal."

"She killed Mr Hogsmith!"

Dad looks peculiarly at me.

"She did what?" he says.

"She killed Mr Hogsmith! He's dead!"

"Kevin, I am sure you are mistaken, there is no way–"

She screeches like a hawk on acid and lunges forward. She goes from standing so still, hobbling from one foot to the other, to running with such speed and determination toward Dad that it takes me a moment to register what's happening.

I hear Dad scream, but I can't see him. She takes him to the floor and mounts him with strength unnatural for a ninety-year-old woman. He tries to push her off but she overpowers him easily – somehow, this weak, ill grandmother with arms like hollow tubes manages to pin him down with such force he can do nothing but wriggle.

I do the first thing I can think of and I grab the spade, running toward Mrs Hogsmith, then pause, wondering – what the hell am I going to do with that spade? What, am I going to smack it over the head of my elderly neighbour – a move that might kill a woman of her age? Or am I going to tap her on the shoulder with it and politely ask her to cease assaulting my father?

"Get off him!" I shout, but I may as well be shouting *llama monkey pie* for all the sense it seems to make to her.

She is growling and choking and shrieking and moaning and her saliva is dripping over Dad's face, old lady spit mixed with blood landing on his forehead, and he tries to move but her veiny hands are on his arms and her yellow, elongated fingernails are digging into his skin.

There is nothing human about Mrs Hogsmith at all, but there's nothing animal either – it's like she's something else. Something worse.

Something much, much worse.

"Aah, get her off of me!"

She sinks her jaw lower, her sharpened dentures

approaching Dad's throat, and I know she's going to bite him, which means he's going to die, and I have no choice.

I lift the spade to the side and use as much momentum as I can to swing it through the air and into her head.

She flies onto her back. Dad scrambles away and ends up in the thistles – sorry, Dad, I mean the *weeds.*

But it isn't over. She sits up, wiping blood from her cheek. The spade may have flattened one side of her head, but it has not deterred her. Whilst her eye may be hanging out of its socket and her ear may be squashed and her cheek flattened, she still manages to push herself up and glare at us with her one working eye.

"Jesus Christ," Dad says. "What is this?"

"I don't know, but Mr Hogsmith is dead in the garden."

She screeches and charges at us again and I have no choice but to lift the spade back and smack it into her face once more. She goes down, her nose flattened, her chin upturned, and her monobrow bloodied.

Still she is not deterred, and she pushes herself to her feet again.

All those other women stand idly on their lawns, shifting weight from one foot to the other, snarling and with blood on their cheeks, turn to look at the commotion. With eyes just like Mrs Hogsmith's, feral and aggressive, they charge at us, running faster than I thought possible.

"In the house!" Dad says, and he sprints back inside. He holds the door open for me and, once we are both in, he slams it behind him.

CHAPTER EIGHT

Dad shuts the door, bolts it, and leans against it, panting. They batter against the door and it shakes, but it seems to hold them – for now, at least.

Dad wipes sweat from his forehead and onto his sleeve. Without saying anything, he rushes to the living room and shuts all the curtains. I take his lead and rush to the kitchen to do the same, and we meet once again in the hallway.

"What on earth is going on?" he asks me.

"How would I know?"

The battering against the door becomes more aggressive. Beneath the sound of its pounding are hisses and growls, moans of agitation, screams at the frustration that they can't get to us.

"We should be safe here," Dad decides.

Just as he says it – in fact, this occurs so promptly after he says this that it's like I made this story up – the ceiling above us rattles.

"What was that?" Dad asks.

I try and think. Did someone break in? Could one of them have climbed the drainpipe?

The ceiling shakes again, prompting a cloud of dust to fall from the lampshade.

Then I remember – Shania was working last night. She'd be asleep upstairs; her room is directly above us.

Though it doesn't sound much like she's sleeping.

"Shania," I say.

"Oh, God!"

Dad goes to run upstairs, but I grab his arm to stop him.

"What?" he snaps.

"Are you sure you want to go up there?"

"Why not? It's my daughter."

"What if she's… like them?"

"Why would she be?"

"I don't know, it just seems like they are all, you know…"

"What?"

"…Women."

Dad frowns the kind of frown he gives me when I say the word *penis* in a joke.

"Really, Kevin, are we being sexist now?"

"It's not sexist, it's an observation."

"Yes, but do you really–"

The ceiling shakes again, and a long, demented growl follows, starting at a high pitch and ending low.

Both of us look to each other, then to the stairs, then to each other. I go to ask Kaylee what she thinks we should do, she is the brave one after all – then I remember she's not there.

Dad and I stare at each other, and I can see him thinking through our options. We know we need to go up there to check on her. It is Shania, after all; we need to know if she's okay, or if she's one of them. We can't leave her.

We are both, however, a pair of wusses.

"Should I get a weapon?" I suggest, but just as I'm about to say *oh shit I left the spade outside* Dad makes his decision and runs upstairs, and I have no choice but to go after him.

He stops outside Shania's room, goes to twist the door handle, then doesn't. Instead, he waits, and listens, putting his ear to the door.

"Shania?" he says.

Nothing.

"Are you in there?"

Still nothing.

"We'd love to know if you are okay?"

Still nothing.

"We're going to watch the Twilight Saga. You like those films, don't you? Would you like to watch?"

Still nothing – I mean, you get the idea by now. She's not going to be okay, is she?

Dad evidently doesn't realise this as he begins to twist the door handle.

"Dad, wait!"

He waves a hand and shushes me before opening the door, slowly, ever so slowly, until the scene is revealed before us.

Shania sits on the floor. Cross legged. In front of the bin. Blood smeared across her cheeks, and her hamster lying half-eaten on her lap.

She turns to look at us, a tiny paw hanging out of her mouth.

I gag.

She leaps up and, with nothing but hunger in her eyes, she charges at us, going from absentmindedly eating to running so quickly I'm not sure we fully register it. Dad tries to shut the door but she shoves an arm in the way and stops us. He swings the door into the arm, hoping she will retract it, but she seems to feel no pain whatsoever.

She kicks the door open and what was a small, sweet woman is now an ominous silhouette filling the door frame.

We run to the stairs, leaping down the steps two at a time, squealing like two overgrown babies.

And, without even realising what it is I'm thinking, my thoughts fire the words across my mind: *my big sister is going to eat us.*

CHAPTER NINE

WE REACH the hallway and run through the living room, through the kitchen, and through the hallway again, circling downstairs like we're in a chase scene from Scooby Doo.

After three or four times circling the downstairs, and close to being sick, Dad opens the door to the bathroom, and pretends to go in, meaning Shania charges in after him.

He shuts the door and presses his body against it. It's not enough; she keeps knocking it open and almost reaches her arm out. He even pushes his body against it, but Shania's strength is still somehow too much.

"Get me something heavy!"

I look around for something, and all I can find is some weird small statue of two people kissing. I think it's a replica of The Kiss sculpture that my parents got for their anniversary – either way, it's of two nude people kissing and is a really strange thing to have in a house where one's children live.

He takes the statue from me and, at the exact moment he manages to shut the door, he slams it down on the handle, knocking it off, leaving Shania with no way to get out of the bathroom, and no downstairs toilet if we need a piss.

"What the hell is going on?" I ask.

Dad, doing what any middle-age conservative does, strides to the television and puts on BBC News.

A frantic news reporter tells us exactly what we expect to hear. It is a man who normally delivers the headlines calmly, but his suit jacket is not on properly, his hair is dishevelled, and he speaks so quickly I have to concentrate to hear what he's saying.

"Our headlines again, in case you have missed it – the government is warning all people, specifically men, to stay indoors. I repeat – all men should not leave the house. It appears that women have turned into mindless cannibals. They have turned on their sons, their husbands, their brothers, their fathers, murdering without prejudice – no man is safe to leave the house for fear of what women may do to them."

The front door rattles.

The bathroom door rattles.

My trembling knees rattle.

"In case you missed it, here is a replay of the interview with the government's lead scientific advisor."

The news cuts from the reporter to a man with oversized glasses, poorly parted grey hair, and an accent that can only be achieved through private education.

"Actually, this is a phenomena we have been studying for some time, and whilst we predicted extra levels of aggression in the female sex, we could not have predicted what has actually happened."

"And what is causing this?" asks the interviewer from off screen.

"We believe – and, again, we still have experiments to

undergo – that this is caused through a mixture of semen and mobile phones."

"How?"

"We have studied how seminal fluid alters the bodies and behaviour of some females in the animal kingdom – it causes female fruit flies to eat more, for example. It changes female behaviour, regardless of which way it is ingested."

"But how is this only just coming about? Women have been ingesting men's semen for thousands of years."

"Well, that's where mobile phone technology comes in. Many men – most men, in fact – carry their mobile phones in their pockets, and this has decreased the sperm count of their semen. Naturally, the body will subsequently need to fill the semen with something else. In this case, testosterone. You are right that more testosterone in semen alone isn't enough, however. We have also seen that radiation from mobile phones causes the blood vessel walls to shrink, allowing potentially harmful substances in the blood to leak into the brain – in this case, an excess amount of testosterone provided by seminal fluid."

"But we are also seeing children affected by this."

"Indeed, they may not have yet experienced semen injected through sexual acts, but they were still created by sperm, and the testosterone around that sperm may well have found a way in."

"This sounds like a far-off theory, I have to admit."

"It does, and at this stage, we are still not ruling anything in or out."

I stand in disbelief. As does Dad. It appears that men have literally fucked women into being mental.

"Are there any women that are immune?" the interviewer asks.

"Now, this is interesting, as it appears this phenomena

affects all women without discrimination, except for one anomaly – one exception."

"And that is?"

"Twins."

"So twins are immune?"

"Not exactly – we are seeing some twins resist, and we are seeing some twins succumb. I believe it is to do with the genetic makeup in twins, although again, I cannot be sure. As it stands, I would imagine that, whilst all women have a 99.999% chance of succumbing to these urges, a twin will have a 50/50 chance as to whether they will be immune."

"A 50/50 chance?"

"Precisely."

As soon as he says this, I think the exact same thing as Dad does:

Kaylee.

EXCERPT FROM WHEN WOMEN ATTACKED PODCAST EPISODE 3 (TRANSCRIPT)

You first appeared on television within hours of the event, didn't you?

That is correct.

You gave us quite the theory.

I did.

It sounded like this was something you'd been studying for quite some time.

(*Sighs.*) Yes, we'd been looking at the increase of aggression in women, and indeed, early studies did suggest that the phenomena was caused by semen and mobile phones and some kind of bizarre interaction between the two.

It was quite a bizarre theory. Ridiculous, even.

Things often are in the early stages. Two thousand years ago, science's early exploration of life told us that the world was flat and that bad weather came from an angry god. Our semen and mobile phone theories were simply the early stage of science's exploration of the... happening. Whatever you wish to call it. And so theories were bound to be quite wild and unsubstantiated.

Please could you remind us of your credentials?

Government lead-scientific advisor, and previously a lecturer in gender studies and environmental influences on biology. I was best known for a paper where I studied the effects of semen on female fruit flies.

And you proposed this theory to the government?

I did.

And they bought it?

(Sighs.) Where are you going with this?

You were removed from your position, were you not?

That is correct.

Why?

Because they found my theory to be nonsense, and they believed they were better proceeding with someone who did not create wild theories. Someone who didn't produce such irrational hypotheses.

How did you feel about that?

The whole thing is irrational, isn't it? Them firing me. My theories. And the concept of all women violently attacking all men.

Was there any truth in your theory at all?

At the time.

And now?

Let's be clear – all we have are theories. No one knows why this happened. No one knows why women just decided to turn into monsters, the concept is beyond rationality!

There's that word again.

What?

Rational.

I think it's an important word to keep in mind. Bizarre events often lead to bizarre explanations.

What do you believe now?

I don't know.

But if we can remove the requirement of evidence, of anyone taking you seriously, or even rationally – what would you say caused it? If you could suggest something with no consequence.

(Sighs. Pauses.) Honestly, no one knows, and I imagine no one will ever know. People will always try to make claims. Same way we don't know how the universe started and so religious fools make wild claims about how our world began. There is no real way to know why this happened, what caused it, or the purpose to its occurring. It is a totally unexpected, inexplicable event, and we should stop trying to analyse it to death as if some kind of sense is going to come out of it. Women went mental, that is all.

And that's the bottom line?

Exactly! Women. Went. Mental.

CHAPTER TEN

I RING, then I ring again, then I ring some more.

Every time I get the same answer:

"Hi, this is Kaylee, I can't come to the phone right now but if you leave a message–"

"Dammit!" I shout, but manage to stop myself throwing the phone across the room.

I lean my head against the wall. Bite my lip. Clench my fists. How did this happen?

How did we go from being so normal, care-free and clueless yesterday, to the end of the world today?

And how the hell am I meant to concentrate on getting through to Kaylee when all I can hear is the rattling of the front door and the screaming coming from the bathroom?

Dad, seeing my frustration, takes over, calling her over and over and over, only to be greeted with the same answer.

As he tries to call, I text her:

Please let us know you're okay, Kaylee. Watch the news and you'll see why. I'm worried about you.

. . .

I'm not sure if telling her to watch the news is redundant, seeing as the mayhem is occurring outside the window.

Oh god, but it won't just be outside the window for her, will it? Even if luck prevails and she is immune, she is in halls of residence. She will have six or seven rooms next to hers, then other sections with plenty more rooms. It will probably be full of these… things. Crazy psycho women, or whatever they are. They will be crowded together like a prison.

I just hope she's seen what's going on quickly enough to shut herself in her room and lock the door. Maybe she left her phone in the communal area and ran, and that's why she's not answering. It's a very real possibility.

Isn't it?

"What do we do?" I ask Dad. I can see him becoming just as agitated as I am with these persistent, unanswered phone calls.

"I don't know, just – let me think."

"I know she's okay."

"What?"

"She's my twin. Honestly, if something had happened to her, I would know."

Dad shakes his head.

"Oh, Kevin. That's not a real thing."

"What?"

"No one is psychic. No one can just know. Not even twins."

"I'm not saying I'm psychic. I'm just saying I'd know."

He smiles patronisingly.

"I'm going to try Mum," he says, and I feel guilty that I haven't tried her yet.

"Where is she?"

"She's working at the nursery today. I'll try her mobile, then I'll try their landline."

As he does this, I crack open the curtains slightly. The women who'd been bashing against the door stop momentarily, and turn their attention to an unsuspecting man running past in his jogging outfit. He's quite athletic, a sculpted body, with a generous bulge in ridiculously tight shorts. He evidently has headphones in, and is so engrossed in his run that he hasn't noticed the chaos around him.

The good-looking fool.

The group of women surround him before he realises what's happening, and it only takes a few swipes of their nails to take him to the floor. He huddles into a ball, cowering; but they don't just kill him. First, they play with him – pulling his top off, and his trousers, grabbing him in places he does not want to be grabbed. He tries to get up and run away, but they catcall him and drag him back.

Once they have humiliated him, Mrs Hogsmith digs her dentures into his throat, Miss Moss who lives opposite tears open his belly with her teeth and relishes the horror on his face as his intestines fall out; and little Felicity, to whom I had given a colouring book for her seventh birthday last week, places her mouth around his unmentionables and rips them off like a stubborn piece of toffee.

"She's not answering," Dad says, and I jump.

I close the curtains, grateful for being distracted from a sight that was both sick and mesmerising.

Dad puts the phone to his ear again, then drops it seconds later.

"Neither is the nursery. No one is answering at all."

A sudden jolt of the bathroom door makes us both yelp.

Shania must be charging against it. It shakes again, and begins to splinter.

I make a decision – a quick one; one I do not think through for risk of changing my mind.

"I'm going to Edinburgh. I'm going to find Kaylee."

Dad looks for a moment like he's going to object, but he doesn't.

"Okay. I'm going with you. But we need to get Mum first."

The door splinters a bit more, breaking enough that we can see Shania's beady eye observing us.

"Okay," I confirm. "How are we going to do this?"

"We have to get to the car. It's in the garage."

The garage is to the side of the house, and we will need to leave the house to get there. How are we supposed to get there without being attacked?

The bathroom door barges open a little more, and Shania is now able to reach her hand out.

If we stay here, she will get us. Out there, the gang will get us.

"What do we do?"

"We run," Dad says. "We get out of the front door and we run."

"Okay."

We edge toward the front door.

Shania punches the bathroom door further open and reaches her head out, licking her lips, her eyes fully dilated, her skin full of veins.

"Will she be okay?" I ask Dad.

He doesn't reply, which is probably a good thing.

"On the count of three," he says.

BANG.

Shania can now reach half of her body out, and she is trying to push herself through the gap she's created.

"One."

She makes it out, her leg still caught in the door.

"Two."

She falls to the floor, free of the bathroom.

"Go now!" I shout. Shania screeches and sprints at us as we run onto the front lawn.

CHAPTER ELEVEN

I SHUT the door in Shania's face. Dad shoves the key in and locks it, then fumbles for the garage key.

We turn, expecting the group of women to run at us. Fortunately, the slam of the door doesn't seem to have distracted them from their meal. There is little left of the runner, but they are still eagerly devouring the last few pieces of flesh.

Dad puts a finger over his lips to signal *shush* – like I need to be told! What, does he think I'm going to blow a foghorn and wave a flag? Just open the garage!

We creep across the grass, past the flowerbed, over the weeds/thorns/whatever-the-hell-they-are, and to the garage door.

Dad places the key in, twists it slowly, and takes it out. He pushes gently against the top of the garage door, then lifts the bottom up, revealing the car.

Once the door is fully up, Dad presses the unlock button on the car keys.

And herein the mistake lies. It isn't the flash of the hazard lights or the click of the lock that does it – it is the *beep boop* that the car responds with that gives us away.

Little Felicity lifts her head, her pigtails swaying in the breeze. She opens her mouth and snarls. Leaps to her feet.

Her face is covered in blood. Her dress is covered in blood. Her knees have blood on them from the expanding puddle of blood coming from the bloody body.

The others lift their heads also, screeching in unison.

"Shit!"

I'm not sure if it's me that says it or Dad, but we do not hesitate to run.

They chase us, and they are quicker, but we are close enough to the car that we can outrun them. I open the passenger door as Dad opens the driver's side, and we throw ourselves in.

Once the doors are shut, Dad presses a button next to the handbrake that locks the doors with a similarly murderous *beep boop* sound.

Mrs Hogsmith leaps upon the bonnet then throws herself on the windscreen. Red puddles trickle from her fists. Her veiny left breast peeps out of a night dress that has seen better days.

Felicity charges at Dad's door with her head and shakes the car upon impact.

Miss Moss tries to open my car door, but can't, so launches her body at the window.

I look at Felicity. Slamming her head again and again against the window that separates the driver from the outside. Leaving imprints of blood.

At Miss Moss pounding her body into my window. Leaving streaks of blood.

At Mrs Hogsmith lifting her fists in the air and bringing them down against the windscreen. Oh, did I mention – she was leaving a fuck load of blood!

I turn to Dad. Frantic. Watching him. Waiting.

Why aren't we going?

He's not even put the key in the ignition. His head is down, like he's sad about something, and this really is not the time.

"Dad, come on!"

He shakes his head furiously, muttering something, and I don't understand why we are not leaving.

A small crack appears on the windscreen, and Mrs Hogsmith aims her fists at it. I'm not too sure if Autoglass are going to be able to fix this one once she's through.

"Dad! Come on!"

He still doesn't move.

Felicity's dented skull creates another crack.

"Dad, let's go!"

Dad lifts his eyes to me. They are damp. He looks despondent.

"Dad?" I say, a little more cautiously.

"I'm sorry…" he whispers.

I look at his hands, at the ignition, and I realise what's happened.

"Dad, where are the keys?"

He doesn't reply.

I look at his hands again. Empty.

"Dad, please answer me – where are the keys?"

He shakes his head.

"Dad, come on!"

"I… I dropped them…"

"You what?"

He lifts a hand and a floppy finger rises, pointing at a space on the ground a few metres in front of the car.

Sure enough, there the keys are.

The keys that we need to turn the ignition.

The keys we need to escape.

The keys we need to ensure we do not experience a violent death from these three crazy bitches.

The crack in the windscreen grows larger. She's almost in.

CHAPTER TWELVE

I AM NO CRIMINAL.

I sweat if I even try to tell the littlest of fibs.

When we were six or seven, Kaylee's hat flew off while cycling and was lost in a lake. She felt so guilty that she decided to tell Mum a dog had ripped it apart. She had barely finished three syllables before I'd blurted out, "It went in the RIVER the RIVER it went in the RIVERRRRRRR!"

But this is no time for ethics. This is a time for hotwiring my Dad's SUV.

Not that I imagine it's unethical to hotwire a car that you own – but still, just the mention of the word *hotwiring* makes me look over my shoulder to check if a hidden police officer is going to leap up from the backseat and arrest me.

Only problem – neither of us have any idea how to hotwire a car.

And, whilst we stare absently at each other, wondering what we are going to do, Felicity is repeatedly banging her head against Dad's window, elongating a crack, Mrs Hogsmith is bringing her fists up and raining them down upon the windscreen that won't last more than another five minutes at most, and Miss Moss is barging at my window with such force that it is also beginning to weaken.

"YouTube!" I blurt out.

"What?" Dad snaps.

"We should go on YouTube!"

"I don't think now is a time for cat videos, Kevin!"

"No, I mean – there must be a video tutorial on how to hotwire a car. I mean, Kaylee used a video on YouTube to learn how to roll her spliff a few years ago."

Dad raises his eyebrows.

"Really, in the circumstances, I think we can forgive her!"

I take my phone out, open the YouTube app, and try to ignore the pieces of glass beginning to land upon my head, trying to ignore the surround sound bombardment, and just focus on the dull, monotone voice of some guy explaining how to hotwire a car, despite him sounding like he's explaining how to set up your train spotting equipment.

"Hi there, my name is Bob, and today we are going to talk you through hotwiring a car."

Felicity screeches as she pounds her head back against the window and I wish Bob would hurry up.

"Remember, never hotwire anyone's car but your own. It is illegal to hotwire another person's car, and you could be prosecuted."

Seriously, Bob, are you kidding me?

"The first thing you need to do is pry open the panels around the key with a screwdriver, and make sure your wire cutters are ready."

I reach under the back of Dad's seat to where he keeps his toolbox and retrieve the screwdriver and wire cutters.

When I lift my head back up, Mrs Hogsmith gives another strike that punches out a large part of the windscreen – big enough that she can now place her face in the hole. I panic, but she can't get anything more than her face in. She sticks her tongue out and tries to reach for me, flicking it like a demented lizard. A bloody heap of drool lands on my knee.

I shove the screwdriver into the panel beside the key as instructed and pry it open.

"Identify battery and starter wires – these are two red wires and two brown wires."

I find them and, as I do, Felicity smashes the window to thousands of tiny shards with the force of her forehead. Despite the little girl's skin now being covered in broken glass and tiny cuts, she is just as determined to reach in and get us.

Dad does his best to push her away, but this young girl's strength seems to be outdoing his.

"As quick as you can!" he tells me.

"Cut the power wires from the cylinder," says Bob, "and connect them by twisting them."

I do as I'm told.

The glass around Mrs Hogsmith's face cracks a little more, and she manages to reach a little further in.

Miss Moss cracks the window with the force of her fists.

My hands are shaking. I'm trying to fiddle with wires and my damn hands are shaking.

"Cut the starter wires from the cylinder and strip ends."

I go to do this and drop the wire cutters.

"Kevin!" Dad whines, now trying to hold off Felicity with both his hands and his feet.

I retrieve them and strip the ends.

"Be careful not to touch the ends as they carry a strong live current, and will shock you."

Dad grabs the wires and thrusts them into Felicity's eyes. She convulses then falls away.

He hands them back.

I put them together and the car starts.

"Brilliant!" Dad says, but the steering wheel won't turn.

"Finally," Bob concludes, "jam the screwdriver into the panel behind the steering wheel to deactivate the steering wheel lock."

I do as Bob says and finally the steering wheel can turn.

Dad shifts into gear and, just as he does, Felicity dives back through the window. Her eyes have been scorched yet, despite her lack of sight, she still manages to grab onto Dad's collar.

Dad drives. Miss Moss falls to the ground. Mrs Hogsmith's body flails in the wind whilst her face remains trapped in the window, but once Dad picks up speed she finally becomes free and floats away like a leaf on a breeze.

Felicity, however, is still holding onto Dad with all her might, screeching in his ear as he holds her off with one hand and spins us around a corner with the other.

I try hitting her. I've never punched anyone before, and I didn't imagine my first time would be assaulting a feral child, but I swing my fist back and launch it into her skull, the top of which has already capsized from the impact of smashing her head against the window.

The power of my punch does very little. It's a little embarrassing, really, but I don't dwell on it.

Seeing a lamp post ahead, Dad drives closer to it, and slams her torso into the lamp post. Her body disappears behind us, but her head remains, and rolls into the space beside Dad's feet. He screams in falsetto, trying to kick it out the way.

I lift her discarded head by the hair, accidentally drop a few pieces of neck and muscle onto Dad's lap, and hurl it out of the window.

Dad tries to wipe down his crotch, but imprints of blood

remain. I can see he wants to complain, but, honestly, cleanliness isn't the priority.

Nevertheless, we are free of them, and en route to the nursery to find Mum.

Or, at least, whatever version of Mum there is left.

CHAPTER THIRTEEN

"She wouldn't kill the kids," Dad insists.

"What?"

"She wouldn't. I know she wouldn't. There's no way. She couldn't do it."

This is what we call denial. We are five minutes away from the nursery where we hope to find Mum, and Dad is insisting that, should she have succumbed to this bizarre cannibalistic state – which I am certain she has, even though I am trying not to think about it – that she would not kill, maim, eat, or harm any of the children in her care.

"These women wouldn't hurt kids," he insists. "None of them would. It's just not possible, not in their nature."

"Why not?"

"It's maternal instincts. Whatever these women are like, their mothering instincts are just too strong. They will kill us, but they will protect the young."

I don't have the heart to tell Dad he's talking nonsense. I don't think these women will discriminate against any victim based on their age, nor their ethnicity or wealth or privilege. Not after what I've witnessed today.

It seems to be only other women they are not attacking.

Dad stops the car at the side of the road. The sign for *Happy Joy Nursery* seems an odd contrast to the eerie silence that surrounds it. Whilst the sign is a mixture of pinks and purples with a smiling face in place of the O in *Joy*, the street smells like smoke, and the door to the nursery seems darker somehow.

"I don't want to do this," I say, without any intention to say it or awareness that it was coming out of my mouth.

"She'll be all right. We'll help her. Once they find a cure, we'll give it to her. We just have to make sure we don't hurt her, however much she tries to hurt us."

"Dad... I'm not sure there is a cure."

"We can't be sure of anything. If there isn't a cure the human race will die out with no women to provide us with young. We have no choice but to find a cure."

"Just because we have no choice, it doesn't mean we will be able-"

"Shut up, Kevin! I am the older one, dammit, and you will listen to me."

I shut up, not because he's told me to, but because he needs me to. He needs to hold onto this false hope; maybe it's all that's keeping him going. You reach a point in your life, when adulthood is beginning and childhood is destroyed, when you realise that your parents are humans who struggle just as much as you do, and that is what he's doing right now – struggling.

"Let's do this," I say, and I get out of the car, expecting him to follow.

I look both ways as I cross the road, which feels a little ridiculous considering we haven't seen a car since we left the house.

I mean, not a car being driven that is. We've seen plenty that have crashed into a building or turned upside down.

We pause outside the door. Listen.

It's too quiet.

I don't like this, and I think we should take a moment to make sure it's safe – but before I can say anything, Dad knocks on the door and shouts, "Hello, is anyone there?"

"Shush!" I say, but stop myself from telling him how stupid that was. The man is in pain, and I want to know if Mum is okay, and I need to get to Kaylee, so I don't delay it any further.

I push the door and it creaks open, displaying a dark hallway.

We walk in, making sure to shut the door behind us. To the right is a kitchen. Ahead, the stairs. To our left, a door covered in children's drawings of poorly scribbled fields, and people with heads too big and skin the wrong colour. The letters of the word *Nursery* are fixed to the door in cut-out cardboard.

I put my ear to the door.

All I hear is slopping. A lot of it. The kind of sound my annoying cousin does when he eats with his mouth open.

I look back at Dad.

"Are you sure you want to go in here?"

"One moment," he says, and walks into the kitchen. When he comes out a moment later, he has a knife for himself, and another that he hands to me.

We exchange a look of confirmation, and I push down on the door handle.

The door opens and I try not to gag.

The room looks like violence threw up on it. Every window, every wall, every floor tile, every table every desk every chair every toy – every damn thing is covered in entrails, whether it be intestines, or muscles, blood; I'm sure I even see an open heart on a table. Female children sit over their male counterparts, feeding on their insides, reaching into their bodies and pulling out bloody objects. For the first time, I'm glad I failed A Level Biology and don't know which parts of the anatomy each child has spread across their cheeks.

"Holy crap..." I whisper.

Across the room, beyond the mass of subdued girls having lunch, is a larger, more adult shaped body.

This adult turns their head. In her hands she holds a leg, digging her teeth into the skin and ripping it off like a piece of fat on a well-done steak.

Her skin is pale. Hair matted. Clothes stained with bodily juices I can't distinguish.

"Mum..."

She looks up.

She sees us.

Her eyes widen.

She stands, curls her fists, and screeches in our direction. All the girls look up and notice us too, changing from subdued to frenzied, joining in with Mum's screeching. Before we know what's happening, a dozen toddlers are charging at us with blood on their face and hunger in their eyes.

CHAPTER FOURTEEN

WE TURN AND WE RUN, as fast as we can – but it is not our bodies that are growing fatigued, it is our minds.

In the split second it takes for me to bolt, everything suddenly hits me. And I mean... what the hell is going on?

My elderly neighbour attacked us.

A seven-year-old girl was decapitated trying to kill us.

We had to trap my older sister, a police officer, in the bathroom so she wouldn't maul us.

And now what? My mum and a group of pre-school girls are eating all the boys in their nursery.

We burst out of the door and back into the street, toward the car. Except, that would be too easy, wouldn't it? That would mean that a part of this was simple! Instead, our car is being hijacked by a group of scantily clad men fleeing out of a nearby house, their clothes ripped, lipstick smeared across their lips. They shake, like something horrific has been forced upon them; like they were being made to do something horrible. They leap into the car and drive away, not even glancing at us chasing them and shouting for help.

We don't have time to consider what to do next as Mum

and the infants clamber out of the nursery, barging one another out the way in their desperation for fresh meat.

We run, and we run quickly.

But I'm faster than my dad, and I find myself having to slow down for him.

Which means they gain on us.

They are too quick.

If I slow down, they'll get us both.

But I am not leaving my dad.

We belt it down the street, sprinting harder and harder. Faces appear at windows, men closing the curtains for fear of being seen, and women leering at us as they lick their lips.

My dad falls further behind me, and further, and further.

And I am forced to stop.

Which is when he seems to realise something.

"I'm holding you up," he realises, his voice melancholic, yet resolved.

"Come on then!" I say.

He shakes his head.

"I can't hold you up. I can't let you die because of me."

"Just come on!"

"No, I'll hold them off. You go."

"What? Don't be an idiot, Dad!"

He shakes his head again.

"I can't outrun them, but I can give you a head start."

"Dad, I–"

"Kevin, please – just let me be with my wife."

And that is when I realise, he is not doing me a favour by staying – I am doing him a favour by letting him.

He stops running, and that is when they catch up with him.

I pause, not wanting to leave, but knowing they will get me too if I do not go.

"Go!" he screams. "Please, just go!"

I run, just as he instructs, not sure whether he's being brave or I'm being a coward.

I keep glancing over my shoulder and, as I do, I see Mum slow down and stop in front of Dad. He places a hand on her cheek, says something sweetly; I can't tell what it is from this far, but it's probably something like "I love you, my dear."

She seems to smile back at him, and she leans in, and for a moment I think they are going to kiss. That is, until she clamps her teeth around his mouth, meaning he isn't even able to scream. She pulls away and spits out a few of his teeth, then bites into his neck and takes him to the ground.

The toddlers surround him. She devours his throat and lets the young ones feed on the rest.

"No!" I cry, not quite registering what I've just seen, but knowing it's awful.

Why did I let him do that?

Why did I not insist?

Why would she do that to him?

Why, why, why – the same question and no answers.

I stop and linger. Not wanting to stay, but unable to go.

As if there's going to be anything left of him to save.

As if not fleeing means I can do something to help him.

One of the girls looks up. Meets my eyes. Licks blood from her lips.

If I stay, I'll be next.

Dad told me to go.

He did that so I could escape.

So I turn and I run.

I keep going until I can no longer see them, and I turn down a street to the left, and keep running. Burnt out cars line the street next to houses with boarded up windows and drawn curtains, and black clouds start to cover the sun with an ominous foreboding that didn't seem to be there this morning.

I am out of breath, I have a stitch, my lungs hurt, but I keep running, not quite sure where I am meant to go, but going there anyway.

I turn down a street full of old-fashioned houses. It looks like the street in *Oliver* where they all sing about what a wonderful morning it is and who will buy their bread and all that shite.

That's when it makes me realise – every movie I've ever seen is bollocks. All the zombie movies I obsess over, all the female action heroes I masturbate to, all the romantic comedies where the guy gets the girl – it's nothing.

No fiction can prepare you for these horrors.

No fiction can tell you what it's like to have the opposite sex make you feel helpless and pathetic – whilst also feeling like you can do nothing to change it.

I stop, bending over, panting.

I'm fairly sure I'm not being followed, so I allow myself a moment.

And I try not to think those words that won't go away:

Dad is dead.

CHAPTER FIFTEEN

I wander.

Not aimlessly, but not with purpose either. It's more of a loiter. I know I should be more aware, that I should protect myself, but I'm not really thinking.

What would you do if you just saw your mum eat your…

I bow my head.

Don't think it. Don't say it. Don't acknowledge it.

I try not to fall apart. I try not to fall to my knees and cry out. I try everything.

I close my eyes, as if that is going to numb the sight, as if that means I don't see my dad's death played in front of me like a cinema screen in my mind, again and again and again.

I stop walking.

Why walk? Where would I go? What would I do?

I just saw my dad…

No. I can't. I can't think it.

My mum, she…

Fuck.

I huff. Shake my head. Turn to my side, and say, "You'd be strong in this situation, wouldn't you?"

Kaylee doesn't reply as she's not here. But that doesn't mean I stop talking to her.

I could really do with her bravery right now.

"You would be the one who makes us keep going, I know you would. I'd fall to my knees, and you would put your hands under my shoulders, pick me up, and tell me to get on with it and deal with the grief later."

I smile a sad smile. She always was the strong one.

"You would tell me it's about survival, wouldn't you?"

She nods. I reach out to take her hand but my fingers just fall through air.

"I didn't have a choice, you know."

I didn't.

"He told me to run."

He did.

"So don't make me feel guilty."

Please, don't make me feel guilty.

I shake my head.

Her absent face looks at me like I did the wrong thing.

I crouch, as if I'm about to heave, but I don't, and my weight drops and I sit cross legged on the floor. In the middle of the street, not a person nearby – nothing but bloody puddles and abandoned vehicles. Sometimes a curtain flickers in a nearby window, but I'm otherwise ignored. Just someone to disregard and leave to die.

"Would you have stayed?" I ask her. "Would you have gone back? Fought them off? See, that's what you don't get – if you went back, you'd have saved him. If I went back, we'd both be dead."

I shake my head. She isn't getting it. She's still giving me that look.

"Please, Kaylee, don't… Just don't…"

My fingers feed through my hair, land at the back of my neck, and I drop my head beneath my arms.

Kaylee doesn't place her hand on my back, but she does. I mean, she's not there, but as far as my imagination is concerned, she does.

She was always the fighter. The one who stood up and made sure she was counted. The one who would tell someone to fuck off while I sat in the background and tried to remain as unnoticed as possible.

A growl comes from behind me. In the distance, but it's getting louder.

The quick patter of bare feet on pavement builds into a crescendo.

"What do you say, Kaylee? Should I just let them get me?"

I lift my head and look at the space next to me, as if it's going to answer.

"What's the point?"

I can smell her now, the woman approaching. Like shit and rotten meat.

Absent Kaylee tells me to stop being a moron. To get off my arse and actually do something that would make her proud. To stop being a coward.

And she's right.

"I know you are. You always are."

I stand.

"I'll get to you. I promise. I will."

Over my shoulder, I see it. A woman who was probably pretty once, but now has missing teeth and clothes soaked in red.

I run.

Slowly, at first, then I pick up speed.

And the run turns into a sprint.

But I have nowhere to go.

Nowhere at all.

Then I hear it. A voice; faint, but definite.

"Hey!"

I look around.

"Hey, over here!"

My head turns to the left. There is a man standing in a doorway, the door slightly ajar, beckoning me.

"In here, quick!"

Is this a trap?

No, it can't be. This is a man. I can trust him.

The woman screeches and I run into this man's home. He shuts the door and bolts it just in time.

CHAPTER SIXTEEN

THE MAN LEADS me through a hallway covered in shadows and into a kitchen. The windows have been blackened out with card and duct tape, and the only light is from candles that illuminate the wooden, rustic kitchen table.

"Please, sit," the man says, and I do so. He gets me a glass of water as I look around. The curtains are a sickly brown, the walls are pale, and there is a bowl of Werther's Originals on the table.

The man's face is white, there are bags under his eyes, and he moves with a wobble. He is old, older than my Dad, probably retired.

Oh, God, Dad…

"Please, drink."

I go to drink, but pause, noticing that there are two other men in the room, sitting at the table with me. One is a man who looks like he's in his forties, and the other a teenager. I notice a picture on the wall of the old man who helped me in here, and an elderly woman who I presume is (or was) his wife. I want to ask where she is, but I don't; I'm too perturbed by the way they are all staring at me. Like they are waiting for something.

"I said drink," the man said.

I go to drink, then hold the water by my lips. Why are they so desperate for me to drink? Why are they so–

Dad.

His face fires across my thoughts again, and I freeze.

He's dead.

Dead.

Dad is dead.

Oh, God.

"Please, you are dehydrated, you must drink," the man says.

I put the glass down.

"In a minute," I say, and I try to figure things out.

All those kids in the nursery. The boys, devoured by their friends. And Mum…

Dad…

Mum killed Dad…

"Please would you dri–"

"In a minute!" I snap.

I look around and their faces are still staring at me, and it is making me feel increasingly uncomfortable.

"Sorry," I say. "I'm just feeling a little… I just saw…"

Saw what, Kevin?

What did you see?

Say it.

Go on.

"I saw…"

You need to say it.

If you are to survive, you need to deal with this quickly, and you need to say it…

"I just saw…"

Come on, dammit!

You know the words, it's not that hard!

"I just saw my dad…"

Yes…

Go on…

"I just saw my dad get murdered by my mum."

Shit.

I did just see that.

Man, I wish I hadn't just said it.

"Drink some water, it will help," the man insists.

They are all leaning toward me, looking from my face to my feet, from my face to my feet, shifting their gaze up and down, up and down. Then I realise – they aren't looking from my face to my feet; they are looking from my face to the glass.

"Why do you want me to drink the water so much?" I ask.

"It will help. Really."

I lift the water to my lips and, if only to stop them staring at me, I pour some into my mouth.

Then I hold it there, not swallowing. Something tastes weird. It's salty.

I look at the water. It's a little foggy.

I spit the mouthful of water back into the glass.

They all tut in frustration, and I stop feeling uncomfortable, and start feeling scared.

"What is this?" I ask.

"Please, just–"

"What is in the water?"

The man sighs. He looks at the middle-aged man across the table from me, who replies, "We'll just have to do it without the Rohypnol. It's fine, she's strong enough."

"Do what? What are you going to do?"

I look back at the glass. The man across the table approaches me, so I pour the contents of the water over the floor to avoid being forced to drink it, then stand and back away.

"What are you doing?"

The older man joins the middle-aged man in approaching, as does the teenager.

"Guys?"

"My wife," the older man says. "We are waiting for the cure. We are waiting to help her get better."

"Cure? Not sure there is a cure."

"In the meantime," the old man says, ignoring my protestations, "she has needs. And she wishes to satisfy those needs."

"Needs? What needs?"

The middle-aged man runs toward me. I turn to run away and the teenager trips me, sending me flying onto my front. The middle-aged man puts his knee against my back and holds my hands behind me.

I kick and thrash and struggle but all three of them together are too much for me. They drag me out of the room and into a bedroom, where they throw me to the floor.

I leap to my feet, but they close the door and I hear a lock turn before I can even try to escape.

I try to open the door. I barge into it, push it, twist the handle. It won't give.

I look around the room.

It is a bedroom. Red satin sheets on a king-size bed. Low lighting. Some kind of weird statue on the cupboard.

I step toward the statue for a better look, because it is really odd. I know what it is, because we learnt about it in my Art A-Level. It is a Jamaican fertility statue. Brown hardwood, a foot in height, featuring a naked man with puckered lips, holding a very large penis that is almost as long as the statue is tall.

I hear a clang. Like chains moving. Scraping along the wooden floorboards.

I look behind me, and there is a door that I assume leads to the ensuite. A woman emerges from it. I recognise her from the framed photo in the kitchen. She must be at least eighty, wearing a nightgown that I am sure would have made her look pretty sexy forty years ago.

There is a chain on her ankle, attaching her to the bed.

She doesn't attack me. Not yet.

But that doesn't set me at ease.

Because I am sure she is about to do something much, much worse.

I run to the door and try to open it again, as if it will unlock when it wouldn't before.

She approaches me from behind and I can feel her stale breath on my shoulder. She puts her arms around me and I push them off, only to find her hand grab my head and smash it into the door in response.

I fall to my knees and her hands start grabbing me all over my body. I try to resist, try pushing her away, but it's useless. She makes me feel dirty and degraded, but the more I show it the more it turns her on, and she overpowers me easily.

I manage to kick her off and I try crawling away from her, but she just grabs my hair and pounds the back of my head against the headboard, again and again, until I'm dizzy.

I kind of wish I had taken the sedative.

She grabs hold of my neck, pulls me to my feet, and throws me to the bed.

That is when she removes her nightgown.

CHAPTER SEVENTEEN

HER FRILLY NIGHTGOWN lays at the foot of the bed, and her pale body, covered in wrinkles and veins, stands over me.

She is smiling, but it isn't the kind welcoming smile of a grandma welcoming you into their home – it is the lecherous grin of a sadistic, conscienceless molester, mentally undressing me over and over and over.

I thought it was bad when they were trying to kill us. Now they are going to do this to me first?

And I emphasise the word *first* – I have no doubt that, once my abuser has satisfied her urges, she will finish me off by battering me to death.

Her leer widens as she crawls over me on all fours. Her short, grey hair hangs over me in greasy clumps, and I choke on the stench of urine emanating from her crotch as her saggy breasts drag her hard, coarse nipples over my chest.

"Please… Please don't… I'll do anything, just stop…"

I don't know why I beg. It's not like she's suddenly going to sit up and go, "Ah, you know what, you're not in the mood, that's fine, let's cuddle instead."

I'm not sure cuddling has even crossed her mind.

I try to get up but her hands grip my biceps and push me down. She is stronger than she should be, and it makes me feel all that much more helpless.

I look around for a weapon. I try to find a knife, or a blade – hell, at this point I'll settle for a pin.

Nothing. It's as if the room has been designed for this.

She takes her hands from my biceps and places one tightly around my neck. She moves her other hand to my crotch and looks at me as if to say, *the harder you struggle the harder you'll suffer.*

Her free hand finds my belt. Undoes the buckle. Undoes the button. Reaches inside. Her skin is ice cold.

I feel humiliated, and she chuckles like she's enjoying it.

I wish Kaylee was here.

I mean, not to witness my molestation – but to help. I don't think I've ever seen Kaylee scared. I wish she could tell me what to do, as I'm clueless.

I close my eyes. Maybe all I can do is just lie still and endure it, numb myself, try to think of other things, just submit and hope it doesn't last too long.

Just as I begin to accept what is about to happen, I see it.

The Jamaican fertility statue.

I lift my hands up to the side of her face. Stroke them gently down her cheek. Look into her eyes the way I used to look into my ex-girlfriend's eyes – the one who dumped me for a guy with a lip ring when she went off to uni.

I pretend to like it; I have to if I'm going to survive.

I have to get to Kaylee.

I have to make sure she's okay.

Which means I have to play along until the right moment.

She seems to appreciate the reciprocation. I smile at her, lovingly, and I lift my lips slightly as an invitation for her to bring hers down to mine.

As our lips meet I feel the stickiness of her saliva and the gunk along the cracks of her lips. She breathes the fishy odour of her breath into my mouth and I repress the need to throw up.

After a few seconds of passionate kissing, her hand loosens around my neck, and I sense my opportunity. I pull my arm back and plunge my fist into her belly.

It doesn't hurt her too much, but it throws her enough to give me the chance to roll off the bed, leap to my feet, and grab the statue.

She charges at me, a face of wrath, furious at the deception.

I hold the statue to the side and swing it with as much speed as I can. The large, unrealistically proportioned penis of the little fellow lodges itself into her cheek.

She falls to the ground. I mount her, rip the statue out of her face, hold it high, and bring it down with all my might, forcing the penis through her throat.

She gags. She splutters. She convulses. Seizing and twisting, opening and closing her mouth like a goldfish, desperate for air.

Her hands scramble at my face, her dirty nails digging into my skin, but she can't breathe, and I just have to wait a little longer for her to die.

I punch the statue, pushing it further into her neck, then pull it out. She wheezes and splutters then becomes limp.

Her eyes don't move. Her body flops.

I stand up and back away, watching her, waiting to see if she'll get up again.

She doesn't.

The horny bitch is finally dead.

I look around the room frantically. Now what do I do?

I leap to my feet and run into the ensuite. Above the toilet is a small window.

I throw the large-penis-dude into the window and it

smashes. I leap onto the toilet, onto the tank, and pull myself up.

The door to the room opens. The men who so skilfully groomed me must have heard the smash. I hear cries of anguish as they find the dead body of the elderly rapist.

I wiggle through the small opening and, just as I'm almost through, I feel a hand around my ankle.

I kick and kick and kick and I feel my heel hit something, and the hand loosens, and I am free to make my way out of the window and drop to the ground.

I land in a puddle on hard cement, and the impact hurts my back. My spine hurts, but I see a pair of eyes through the smashed window and I know I can't wait around.

I push myself up and run until I'm clear of the house.

EXCERPT FROM WHEN WOMEN ATTACKED PODCAST EPISODE 4 (TRANSCRIPT)

Thank you for joining us, Matthew. I understand this is a tough subject for you to share with us.

It's okay. Really, it's fine. If I can help someone with my story, then… Well, then it's worth it, I guess.

That's really very brave of you.

Thank you.

If you'll allow me, I'm going to get to the point straight away. You are a victim, and your mother the perpetrator, is that right?

I prefer not to call myself a victim. I'd rather be known as a survivor.

Of course.

And yes, my mother was my abuser.

What did your mother do to you, Matthew?

(Pause.) Well, it's… I dunno. I never saw it coming. She was a kind mother, liked by everyone, then when this was all happening, she just… she came into my room. She just stood in the doorway, the light behind her, and her silhouette looked… different. She didn't have the same posture. She was… *(Sniffs.)*

Are you okay?

Fine.

Do you want to stop?

No. It's fine. Just… Give me a minute, okay?

Okay. In your own time.

(Pause.) She shut the door. My dad was out, and she didn't need to, but she still did. Just in case. Then she walked in, stood at the end of my bed and… and told me to stand up.

Did you know what she was about to do?

Of course not. Who would ever imagine that their mother could do that to them?

Not many people, I imagine.

She stroked my face. Slowly, with a light touch. I suppose she thought it was a loving gesture, but… there was nothing loving about it.

What happened next, Matthew?

She – she – she told me to take my top off. I questioned her and she hit me, slapped me, hard, across my cheek, and I was so taken aback and… I suppose most people would say that, in this position, they would not have done it.

I don't think anyone can know what they would have done in your position.

They wouldn't. People would probably say they'd have run out or run away or hit back or – or whatever. But they can't say that. They don't know. And I… I feel so ashamed.

You shouldn't feel ashamed.

It's nice of you to say, but I didn't fight back, or do anything. She scared me and, although there was no force, there was no pinning me down or making me, I still did it, and I…

Your mother should have known better.

But I let her. *(Pause.)* I let her…

CHAPTER EIGHTEEN

It's probably been half an hour since I started running and, as someone who only ever runs if I hear an ice cream van, I am out of breath and out of energy. I manage to dodge most women I pass, either because they are feeding on some helpless bloke on the ground, or because I see them in time and sneak behind them. Eventually, I come across a petrol station and slow down, ignoring my stitch, and decide this will be a good place to stop.

The petrol station is deserted, but I remain cautious. As I open the door, a pointless ding welcomes my presence.

It's empty.

Well, empty of the living, anyway.

An unrecognisable corpse lies in the chocolate aisle with his chest open and his ribs bent apart. I wonder where his intestines, liver and heart is – then I feel a sudden need to be sick, and the thoughts leave me as I run to the bathroom products and throw up over a well-stocked shelf of sanitary products.

There are more bodies by the magazines and splatters of blood on the floor, so I walk in the opposite direction, toward the drinks, and take a bottle of water. I feel guilty for not paying for it, then I remind myself that, considering there is a bunch of dead dudes on the floor, a 35p bottle of water is probably not that big a deal.

I drink it and I relish it and I've never really considered how great water is. I drain the bottle in seconds.

I try to open the bathroom door but it's locked, so I go to the vegetables, open my fly, and pee on the broccoli. I figure that, once the end of the world arrives, broccoli will be the last thing people try and salvage, so this is the best place to do it.

You may think it is vulgar of me to wee on the veg, but just ask yourself, how many times do you watch a film or read a book and they never urinate? It's unrealistic. I remember watching Jack Bower in 24, where every episode takes up an hour of the same day, wondering – when does the guy go to the bathroom? We've just watched him for 24 hours and he never needs to go. It's unrealistic. Hence why I take this opportunity to go; sometimes, even us fictional characters need to relieve ourselves.

I finish, shake off and zip up, and that's when I hear the bell chime over the door.

I drop to the floor, avoiding the few splashes that landed on the tiles, and I creep toward the lettuce where I am better concealed.

"Only get a few wee snacks for the drive – nothing too heavy. I want to get home."

It's a male voice, and that provides me with a little relief – then again, remember what a group of men just did to me. It won't hurt to retain a little bit of caution.

"Okay, Dad," says a younger voice.

They both have strong Scottish accent. They are going *home* – is that Scotland?

If so, they are going in the direction I need to go to find

Kaylee. In which case, I need their help. So, knowing they will find me, I decide I may as well reveal myself.

"Hello," I say, and stand.

A man, possibly in his forties, instinctively points a knife toward me.

His son, maybe around twelve or thirteen, pauses at the other end of the shop.

"It's okay, laddie," the father says. "I'll deal with this one, you go ahead."

The man steps closer, pointing his blade in my direction, keeping his eyes fixed on me.

I hold my hands up.

"Please, I don't mean any harm," I tell him. "I'm a man."

It feels like a stupidly obvious thing to say, but I say it anyway.

"What do you want?"

"I just came in here for some food."

"Oh, aye?"

"Then I heard your accent, and you said you're going home – are you going to Scotland?"

"What's it to you?"

"My twin sister is in Edinburgh. I'm trying to get to her. The rest of my family are…"

I struggle to say the word *dead*. Dad crosses my mind, as does Mum, as does Shania, and I push their faces deep, deep down.

"And you're trying to hitch a lift?"

"That's right."

"Well you can bugger off. How do I know you aren't going to hurt my boy?"

I wouldn't. Please, I understand you want to protect your son. My dad just…"

Again, I can't say it. But I have to. I force myself. It may be the only thing that will convince him.

"My dad just sacrificed himself so I can live, so I can get to her."

"Dunno. You could be telling me any kind of fib."

"Why would I lie?"

"I don't know, but I've seen a lot of things today that have surprised me."

"I think we all have."

The man says nothing. Just watches me. Studies me.

"Please. I – I have no other way."

He studies me a moment longer, then drops the knife.

"Fine. But the first sign of trouble, and I'll cut your throat, you understand?"

"I understand."

"I am not risking my son's life for a second."

"I respect that. I won't be any trouble."

"Fine. Best be on our way."

He leads me to the door and calls out to his son.

"Are you coming lad?"

"Yes Dad, I'm just getting the broccoli."

CHAPTER NINETEEN

We get into a people carrier – a Citroen MPV. The father drives, whilst his son sits in the passenger seat and I sit in the back.

I can't quite decide what to make of this guy. He looks older than he is, with bad skin and crooked teeth, and a cap that covers his thinning hairline. He seems like the kind of guy whose ego would be severely damaged by these women being able to overpower him – as if their audacity to stand up to him is more offensive than the murder and mayhem they have caused.

His son also looks a little rough, despite being so young. He chews with his mouth open but I see no gum. He wears a grey tracksuit, has a line across the side of his hair, and walks with a bit of a swagger.

The motorway is relatively easy to drive across. There are a lot of abandoned cars, mostly in the hard shoulder, though a fair few are scattered across the road. Still, the man is able to swerve around the cars easily.

I lean my head back and sigh, take a moment to breathe,

finally able to have a moment to contemplate what's happened.

Could there be a cure?

Could Shania and Mum be saved?

I try not to think about Dad, but I can't help it. I wonder if he was conscious while they opened him up … I wonder if he had to watch himself die…

No, stop it. I can't. I just can't.

Maybe later. Maybe once this is over. But not yet.

I focus on the only person left. The one I am determined to get to. Kaylee.

I take out my phone and try her again. Put it to my ear, and listen to her phone dial out, and her answer machine respond.

I try, then try again. Still nothing.

So I text her instead:

I'm coming to Edinburgh to get you. Please get somewhere safe. And please let me know you are okay.

Is her lack of reply a bad thing? I mean it can't be good… Then again, she could have lost her phone, or she could be hiding and it ran out of battery – there is no way of knowing.

In a way, I hope I don't make it to Edinburgh. That way, I can always live with the possibility that she is okay. I don't know what I'd do if I arrived to find that she's…

No, this is Kaylee. I must get to her.

I go onto Facebook to see what people are saying. My newsfeed is full of posts by men from last night, but not much from today.

. . .

Had to cover myself up after some woman tried following me. Maybe I shouldn't have gone out so late at night...

Dad says I should change what I wear and stop being so boring #lifeproblems

What the fuck is going on? #bitchesbecrazy

I go further back, trying to find posts by women, giving me some kind of idea when this started. There are a few from two or three days ago, and the first post I find includes a picture of a random man's crotch:

Look at the dick on that! #yumyum #gimmegimme #bitchbetter-havemymoney

Brad Pitt is such a minger. Don't know what everyone's on about.

Now this is a video that shows us how it should be done... #lovemesomecock

I click on the video in the last status. It opens a video on a porn website with the title *Gang Bang in the Locker Room*. A man sits on his knees, surrounded by at least six or seven women. He licks the clit of one woman, then the other, then another. One of them starts fucking him from behind as he does this. Another squirts on his face and tells him to keep his eyes open, slapping him when he doesn't.

It makes me feel a little sick. I turn it off.

I notice that my phone's battery is at 7%. There is a USB port beside my seat.

"Hey," I say to the two in the front. "Do either of you have an iPhone charger?"

The boy passes me one, and I plug my phone in.

"So what's your name?" the dad asks.

"Kevin. What about you?"

"I'm Patrick. This is Clyde."

The boy, Clyde, gives a nod.

"So where did you say you're headed?" Patrick asks.

"Edinburgh."

"Oh, aye. Why there?"

"It's where my twin sister is."

"Sister? You going after a woman?"

"Have you seen the news?"

I don't know why I ask; this man evidently does not watch the news. Unless it's a television show with a pair of tits or a bunch of inbreds arguing, then I imagine he's not interested.

"It says that twins can be immune," I tell him. "Something in the genetic makeup means they have a 50/50 chance."

"You're kidding yourself. They are all the same. All of them."

"We can't know that."

"Can't we? You met one that hasn't tried to eat you? Tried to touch you up? Treated you like shit? Eh?"

"I suppose not."

"No you have not. They are all the same. The lot of them." He stares at me in the rear-view mirror and asks, "You lost anyone?"

I bow my head. I could lie, but I don't. I'm not sure why.

"Yes," I say.

"Who?"

"My mum and sister are like them... and my mum killed..." Come on Kevin, just say it. "...My dad."

"That's shit. Still, I bet most of the men who've been murdered have been killed by their other half."

"Yeah..."

"Clyde lost his brother a day ago. And his mum."

"Oh, I'm sorry."

"Chet was his name. May have seen him in the news; some whore who likes to throw it around accused him of raping her. Pure shite, of course."

"I bet."

I absolutely do not believe it is pure shit, but I'm hardly going to tell that to the guy who's driving me to Edinburgh.

"Then the bitch showed up and killed him," Patrick continues.

"I'm sorry to hear that."

"Stupid slut. Shouldn't have been offering herself to everyone. What did she expect? Chet would have seen that and assumed she wanted it."

I frown. Bite my lip. Say nothing.

"I cut her throat myself for that," he says with a smug smile. "Should have done it long ago. I've always looked forward to the day I can give these bitches what they deserve."

An uncomfortable silence settles. I shift nervously. Trying not to let my face show my disapproval. I can see his eyes glancing at me in the rear-view mirror, and I do not want to annoy him, so I divert my attention to my phone. I look up Chet. Numerous articles appear, and I click on the first.

The article shows how this woman, who had kissed another man on the same night in question, had drunk so much she could barely stand, and instead of helping her back to her room, Chet took her back to his. He was found not guilty – seeing as she could not remember the incident, the jury decided there was no way she could remember whether she gave consent or not.

I don't suppose Patrick might concede that a drunk woman perhaps can't give consent…

It's best I just stay quiet.

Don't engage.

Don't argue.

Just let it go. Smile. Be grateful for the help.

"We stop in an hour for petrol," Patrick announces, then turns to me and asks, "You got a weapon?"

"A weapon?"

"Aye, like a knife or something."

I shake my head.

"Fucking useless, ain't you?" Patrick says, and I get the feeling that, if the women don't kill me, this guy might.

CHAPTER TWENTY

We drive in silence for the next half an hour or so, and I realise it's getting dark. We are now well into the evening on what is the longest day of my life.

"What's this?" Patrick says, slowing the car down.

I lean forward, trying to see what he's talking about. There is someone in the road. It looks like a man, but I can't be sure.

Patrick begins turning the car to avoid him, and I can't quite believe he's just going to leave this wounded man in the middle of the road.

"We need to stop and help him," I say.

"Don't fucking tell me what to do."

"Dad," Clyde interjects, "he might be hurt."

Patrick huffs. On the request of his son, he pulls the car over, but doesn't kill the engine.

"Clyde, stay in the car," Patrick says, then turns to me. "You, come with me."

"Really? I don't know if–"

"I said come with me."

Patrick takes out a large hunter's knife, and I wish I

hadn't left the Jamaican fertility statue behind. He steps out of the car, and I follow, staying behind him.

Slowly, we approach. The closer we get, the more I can make out the body. It is still twitching, but the eyes are closed. I can't tell if he's dead or hurt.

Patrick stops by the body, but I keep my distance. He crouches down, places two fingers on his neck, then scowls at me.

"Stop being a pussy and come over here," he tells me, and I approach cautiously.

"Come on," he insists, waving his arm, and I assume he's asking me to crouch next to him, so I do.

I don't know why I'm so apprehensive. I mean, it's a man, and there doesn't appear to be anyone else around.

It just feels wrong. Like this is a bad idea.

"Looks like he was gutted, see," Patrick says, indicating a line across the torso.

The body twitches again, and just as I think the man might still be alive, a rat emerges from the body's belly.

It makes me jump. Patrick doesn't even flinch.

"Fuck off, go on!" he says, waving his arm at the rat, who scampers away.

I look up and down the body, repressing the need to gag, and that's when I realise – I know this man. I recognise him. Who is he?

The face is familiar...

Oh my God. It's Bill Field. The husband of that woman Mum was obsessing over.

"Poor little shite," Patrick says. "Had his torso split open."

Again, I get a feeling like something is wrong. The way he's just lying in the middle of the road... It just feels unnatural...

I mean, I know disembowelling a guy is fairly unnatural –

but it's the way he's positioned, it's as if he's been placed there deliberately...

That's when I realise – the torso is open, but the contents of his body remain. I've seen these women eat and they don't leave anything. They open up the bodies and consume all of the insides.

Why was this guy's body parts still intact?

"Patrick, this isn't right."

"Tell me about it. Bitches that did this ought to be shot."

"No, that's not what I mean – why are his intestines still there? His heart? Why hasn't whoever did this finished him off?"

"Because they just wanted to hurt the doaty sod. That's what they are, nasty little bitches, just hurting for no reason–"

"No, I don't believe that – they are feeding."

"Feeding? They don't feed. They just kill."

"But they–"

That's when it hits me like a punch in the gut – this body has been placed here intentionally.

But why?

"Oh my God," I say. "It's bait."

"Eh?"

"He's been left here as bait."

I stand, turn, about to sprint to the car, but stop. There is something in my way.

"Patrick..."

"What?"

"Patrick..."

"What!"

He stands, about to launch into a verbal tirade against me, then stops, staring at the same thing I am staring at.

From the shadows, she emerges. Helen Field.

Activist.

Inspirational, charitable woman.

Honourable, wonderful person.

And discreet abuser of her husband.

She just seemed so… lovely. So nice. She helped so many people. It's hard to think that she may have been a nasty piece of shit all along, just helping people to gain access to those she can abuse.

"What do we do?" I ask, but Patrick ignores me. He's too focussed on Helen approaching, on all fours, hunched and growling, ready to pounce.

This woman is clever. She's not like the other women who chased me – she's taking her time to hunt us. Everything she does is deliberate. Intentional. A perfect predator, waiting to catch us out.

"We run for the car," Patrick says.

"We need to be cleverer than that."

"Clever? Who's being fucking clever?"

"She's hunting us, Patrick–"

"Shut up. We run for the car."

"But–"

"Now!"

Patrick runs.

I hesitate and, before I know it, I'm on my own, and Patrick is in the car with the door shut.

I'm stuck rigidly in place, looking into the eyes of the woman who's probably about to kill me.

I go to run, but Helen growls and crosses my path.

She is smart. She doesn't go for the one with the knife. She waits for the easier target.

I go to run again, but it's no use; she's blocking my path.

Then she leaps, too quick for me to react.

She dives on me and takes me to the ground.

Patrick begins to drive.

CHAPTER TWENTY-ONE

You prick, Patrick.

You absolute prick.

You're about to drive off without me, aren't you?

You're about to speed away!

But he doesn't. He travels slowly, the car inching forward.

What is he doing?

He shouts something at me but, due to the psychotic beast on top of me, I don't quite hear him.

She has me pinned down by my neck and I can no longer breathe. Blood drips from her mouth onto my forehead, and I feel it running down my nose and meeting my lip as I try for breath that doesn't come.

Patrick is still shouting something, the car is still moving slowly forward, but I have no idea what it is.

I try to reply, "I can't hear you," but I can't speak.

Helen decides to strangle me with one hand. You'd have thought this would make her easier to fight off, but it doesn't. She is still too strong and it is just as impossible to release myself from her grasp.

She uses her other hand to trace her finger down my body. Down my shirt, to my navel, to my belt.

Patrick shouts again.

For Christ's sake, I can't hear you!

Finally, he sticks his head out of the window and shouts louder.

"Lift her head up!"

"What?" I gasp, but no noise comes out,

"Lift her head up and to the side so I can get her!"

I take a moment to realise what he's suggesting, but I get it.

The car edges closer.

I lift my hands up and push at her face. She tries to bite my finger, but I avoid it. I put my hands around her throat and try strangling her, but it just prompts a patronising smile. She is dominating me in every way.

With a determination to be stronger, I push both my hands against the side of her chin and move her to the side. She resists, but she budges a little bit.

I choke. I can't breathe. I get a head rush. I feel dizzy.

I'm running out of time; I'm bound to fall unconscious soon.

Her other hand now has me, all of me, and she is grabbing and rubbing and twisting in ways that I'm sure she might find pleasurable if done to herself, but feels horrific to me.

The car approaches.

I try pushing her. She's too strong.

So this is what it's like to die…

And I hear her, Kaylee, talking to me, and even though it's in my mind it feels like she's right next to me, teasing me like she often would.

"Would you get over yourself?" she says. "You are such a little girl…"

You're right, Kaylee.

I need to stop feeling sorry for myself.

With a burst of adrenaline and as much strength as I can muster, I twist my body and push her head to the side.

The car picks up speed, and I hold Helen there until the bumper smacks into Helen's head and the wheel narrowly misses mine.

Her head rolls away, and her body flops on top of mine.

I shove it off, take a large breath, and lay there, panting.

Patricks grins down at me.

Why is he grinning?

"Put your wee todger away," he says, chuckling.

I look down, not realising that Helen had completely unveiled me. I pull my trousers up and go to my knees, still taking in as much air as I can.

"I thought you were about to leave me," I say.

Patricks shrugs. "So did I."

I remain in this position, coughing, breathing, taking in oxygen, gathering myself

"I thought I was going to die…"

"Hurry up and get in the car," Patrick says. "We got a long drive."

I almost thank him for the sympathy, but decide sarcasm isn't the best thing to give to a man who could have easily driven away, but instead chose to save my life.

I use the car to pull myself up, looking at Helen's detached skull, the red entrails leaking from it, and her eyes that still stare at me with a strange kind of leer.

I take a run up and kick her head, expecting it to fly away like a football.

It doesn't. It barely budges, and it really hurts my toe.

Not looking at Patrick for fear of a large grin and huge amount of teasing at my manliness, I return to the car and say nothing as we drive away.

CHAPTER TWENTY-TWO

ALL I CAN THINK about are the dead eyes of Helen Field, still open and still judging me.

She was a deceitful woman, who had convinced us of her noble intentions and used her own husband as bait – but that isn't what's bothering me.

Her ravenous eyes looked so much like Mum's as she...

As she...

I hate Dad for telling me to go on.

And I hate myself for listening to him.

He was an idiot for sacrificing himself so I could live.

Why the hell did I let him?

Why did I not go back?

I wonder if he suffered, but who am I kidding – of course he suffered. He was eaten alive by his own wife and a group of psychotic pre-schoolers.

What about Shania... might she still be okay?

I'm in denial. I know I am. Of course she's not.

I really hate Helen Field. I was doing so well. I was keeping it all inside, saving it up for later, ignoring the thoughts and the memories and the incessant nagging and refusing to think those words, those dreaded words, those three words that might release me but would probably destroy me.

They. Are. De–

I can't.

I'm sorry, I just can't.

My stomach feels sick. I feel its contents lurch. I haven't eaten anything, and it's just blood and acid, but it gurgles and swims around my belly and gets ready to shove itself up my throat.

"You okay, lad?" Patrick asks, looking at me in the rear-view mirror. I didn't know I was being watched.

I nod.

"You're looking a wee bit pale."

"I, er… I'm not feeling so good."

"Well don't you be sick in my car, don't want the seats ruined."

I frown at him.

Don't be sick in his car?

My family are… *you know...* and he's complaining about a little mess on his upholstery?

The whole world has gone to shit, the human race could be coming to an end, and every woman we have known or loved has turned into a rabid monster, and he is moaning about the possibility of a little mess in his car?

I hate him. I want to lash out, but I'm not really a lashing out kind of person. I'm more of a silent fury kind of person. Passive aggression or staying quiet is more my style.

"You sure you're alright? Do I need to pull the car over?"

I shake my head.

"We need petrol anyway, we'll be stopping at the services in five minutes."

I nod.

I feel cold yet sweaty.

Manic yet motionless.

Empty yet full.

I was so hell-bent on surviving that I hadn't stopped to think, and now…

Now it's all coming back.

My entire body lurches as I gag.

I wind down the window, stick my head out, and projectile vomit into the wind. The smaller pieces of regurgitation float on the wind before splattering against the ground.

"Oh, fuck's sake," declares Patrick. "You got it on the outside of the door. Now I'm going to have to go in the car wash."

I avoided the upholstery… I managed to open the window and keep it all out of the car… And he complains about that?

I want to scream at him, *what do you want from me?*

But I don't.

Like I said, confrontation isn't really my style. Sitting silently and ruminating is more my way of dealing with anger.

The services approach, and Patrick pulls in.

I feel myself about to be sick again, and put my head out of the window, but this time I manage to suppress it.

"Let's get something to eat first," Patrick says, and stops in a parking space.

The entire place is dead. Cars are abandoned, some left in their parking space and some on the grass verges with their doors still open.

There is no sign of life – not to say that there isn't anybody here, but there does not appear to be.

I still know that it is foolish to go off on my own, that there is no way to know for sure that I won't be attacked – but I don't care. Right now, in this moment, I need to be alone, and I need to let it out, and I do not want Patrick and Clyde around to witness it.

"I'll be right back," I say, then add, "toilet."

I get out of the car. Sprint. Ignore the perplexity on Patrick and Clyde's faces. Ignore the eerie silence that can only mean danger. Ignore the pain of my loss, just for a moment longer.

I run through the services, not seeing anyone else but not staying around to look, and make it to the toilets, where I enter a cubicle, sit on the toilet lid, and cry like I've never cried before.

CHAPTER TWENTY-THREE

It all comes out.

Everything.

Dad. Running. Helping me. Telling me to go on. Getting eaten.

Shania. Chasing us through the house. Trapping her in the bathroom. Her attempt to escape. To kill us.

She wanted to kill us.

She tried to get out, bash through the bathroom door, all so she could maim or torture or mutilate us in whatever way her instincts would have dictated.

Mum, eating Dad. The strange way she told me what to wear last night. The odd behaviour I should have thought more about, but like most instances of peculiarity, I just accepted it.

While some people might question something that feels off, I just come to terms with it quickly.

Even in this new world, the fact that women are trying to kill us… I haven't even considered just how messed up that is…

And my family is gone. They are either dead or left to carry on killing.

I wonder if Mum's hurt many other people?

Or if a man has killed her in self-defence?

Honestly, I'm not sure which would be worse. If she's still alive, or if she's been put out of her misery.

But what if they could be cured?

I scoff.

A cure.

Deluded hope, that is.

There is no cure. There is just death.

I take some toilet paper and dab my eyes. My crying starts to slow down. I think the worst has passed.

Then I picture Dad's face as I ran away and it all comes pouring back out.

I hold the tissue to my eyes and cry into it.

I need to make sure I don't look like I've been crying when I walk out. Patrick will hardly think kindly of giving a lift to what he will surely refer to as a 'pussy.'

Then I remember – the reason I'm travelling with this scumbag and his son.

Kaylee.

I do have family left.

The news report... It said twins have a 50/50 chance of survival...

She could be fine.

Then again, she might not be.

I take out my phone. Still nothing from her.

I try calling again, even though I know she won't pick up.

"Hi, this is Kaylee, I can't come to the phone right now–"

I hang up. Text her again.

Please let me know you're okay.

. . .

Just because she doesn't answer her phone or reply to text messages doesn't mean anything. She might have had to run or hide before she could grab her phone.

She is all the family I have left. I must not fail her. Dad would want me to find her. Hell, even Fucked-Up-Shania and Fucked-Up-Mum would want me to get to Kaylee.

And I need to get to her.

At the moment, my memories of childhood and the closest friendship two people can have are lovely pieces of nostalgia. If I don't find her, the memories will become nasty and poisoned and will do nothing but conjure pain. I don't want that. I want thoughts of her to remain happy.

Which means I have to find her.

And, whether you believe in twin intuition or not, I know, I truly know, deep in my heart, that she is okay.

I would sense it if she wasn't, I'm sure of it.

Yes, maybe it's bullshit – but women turning psycho and killing everyone seemed like a bizarre concept yesterday, so hey, why not have a little faith.

So I stop crying.

I have to stay strong.

For Kaylee.

For my family.

I finish wiping my eyes. Place the tissue in the toilet, then take some more toilet paper and wipe the last bits of dampness.

I go to flush, ready to leave, but stop.

A creak echoes.

I freeze. Remain completely still.

It could just be Patrick and Clyde.

But I know it's not. There are no voices asking if I'm in here, and no stomping with their arrogant footsteps.

No, these footsteps are slower. More sporadic. They drag along the floor. Inhumane, chaotic steps.

These are the footsteps of an animal.

One of them is in here, I know it.

And I am completely alone with nowhere to go.

CHAPTER TWENTY-FOUR

MEANWHILE, as I'm shitting myself, Patrick and Clyde are sliding over the McDonalds counter and helping themselves to cheeseburgers that had been readied for customers and subsequently abandoned. They have become immune to the sight of discarded male bodies, such as the ones that lay around the open seating of the services – not that Patrick was ever really that bothered by it in the first place – and search for food without giving them a second glance.

(*And, yes, I realise this story is in first person, and that there is no way I could know what is happening in a different part of the services despite my narration of the events – but, honestly, if the consistency of perspective is really what you take issue with in the potential realism of his book, then I think you have a problem.*)

Patrick shovels his third cheeseburger into his mouth and looks for another. Clyde, however, seeks out his next box of chicken nuggets.

(*By the way, I just realised I was a bit harsh then. I do apologise. We're still friends, right? Oh, God, this is going to play on my mind for ages now...*)

Patrick, in need of a drink, meanders to the milkshake

machine, puts his mouth beneath it, and pours strawberry milkshake directly into his mouth.

Clyde, seeing the fun in this, does the exact same thing with the ice cream machine, twisting and twirling long squirts of McFlurry into his mouth until he has ice cream pouring down his cheek.

(*Look, I'm sorry to keep interrupting the story, but this is really bothering me now. I shouldn't have said that, I... oh man, the thing in the bathroom is making noises. Maybe there are bigger issues.*)

Within ten minutes, having also descended on Burger King and Costa, they are full up on burgers and paninis.

Patrick goes into Marks and Spencers to find a can of cider. As he does this, Clyde pauses, and looks around, considering how eerily quiet it is.

"Where's the other guy gone?" he says. "What's his name?"

"Not sure – Keith? Kayla? Karla?"

"Keith is a gross name."

"That's what I thought."

Patrick sniggers, downing the can of alcohol with such speed that he can't help but dribble some onto his t-shirt. He doesn't notice.

Clyde, however, being the more conscientious of the two – although that still doesn't mean he was particularly conscientious at all, really – looks around.

"Where did he go, though?"

Clyde also realises that there are no women in this place, which is odd, as this would have been one of the most populated places when they began their attack.

Patrick looks around. Listens. Where has this lad gone?

"Eh, kid?" He looks to his son. "What was his name though; was it Keith?"

"Think so."

"Keith, you there?" he shouts, then turns to his son again. "Weren't it Kevin?"

Clyde shrugs.

Patrick realises he doesn't really care that much, and goes to call out – but doesn't. A flicker of light distracts him.

He holds his hand out to Clyde, telling him not to move, and watches. Listens.

Something moves near the newspaper stand. The headlines all show yesterdays' news, stuff about the hot weather we'd been having or about Christmas sales coming too early – you know, stuff that in no way matters at all.

Clyde edges forward.

"What is it?" he whispers

Patrick walks ahead of Clyde, peering, trying to see what's there. "Eh, Karla, that you?"

Something is there. Lurking.

Patrick takes out his hunter's knife.

From behind the newspapers, she emerges. Hair greasy and bloody, face snarling, body hunched. Her brown skirt is half-ripped – not that she'd care.

Behind the counter in M&S, another noise announces itself. A blond. One that Patrick would have previously wolf-whistled at – but now, he does everything he can not to attract her attention.

Behind them, footsteps. Over Patrick's shoulder is a disgruntled obese woman wearing a McDonalds t-shirt.

"Shit, you think she's pissed that we stole the food?" Clyde says.

Another emerges from Costa. Another from behind a table where she'd been feeding on a body. Another from Costa, and another from between the food aisles in M&S, and another and another.

Patrick flexes his finger over his knife, but he knows it's not enough. They are completely, utterly surrounded.

CHAPTER TWENTY-FIVE

I LIFT my feet and place them on the rim of the toilet. I don't know whether these women have the intelligence to check for people's feet, but I don't take the risk.

I breathe as silently as I am able – which is not that quiet. I don't know if you're ever tried to breathe silently, especially when you're panting from fear, but it is bloody difficult.

The shadow passes the gap below the cubicle door. Her footsteps are erratic. She grunts every few seconds, like an old man coughing but higher pitched.

I close my eyes. Pretend there's no one there. Whatever it takes to stay calm.

I've never been too good at figuring out what to do in a crisis. That was always Kaylee's job. I'd panic, and she'd fix it, like when my girlfriend dumped me a few months ago, I had to listen to everyone's constant advice. Mum told me about when she was young and split up with her first love, Dad gave me the normal cliches of "it's better to have loved and lost than never to have loved at all" (which is complete bollocks by the way), and Shania told me to grow a set of balls and deal with it. Kaylee, however, said nothing. She didn't need to. There was nothing to be said. She knew how I was feeling, so she needn't ask. She just came into my room as I sat on the edge of the bed, my head in my hands, gave me a brief hug, then sat next to me. Not saying a word. She sat there for ages, waiting until I was ready to move, and binge-watched Netflix with me.

Or, when I was bullied by Herbert Phillips, a delinquent I was unfortunate enough to go to school with, and I felt like going home and crying every night. His bullying was subtle and, in isolated incidents, seemed like I was being petty in getting upset. He'd draw a picture of a girl on the front of my exercise book to insult my masculinity. He'd exclude me from games of football, telling everyone not to pass to me or involve me in anyway. He would spread rumours about me on social media, but subtle ones – like that I fancied a certain teacher, or came onto a girl in class that no one liked.

Kaylee didn't take his shit, however. She found out what he was doing, marched right up to him the next day and, as he laughed at the hilarity of a girl standing up for her brother, she punched him in the face.

He never told a teacher. In fact, Herbert Phillips never told anyone.

But he never, ever messed with me again.

And now Kaylee is in Scotland. Away from me. Possibly dead, possibly not.

And I am trapped in a bathroom stall with some psycho bitch ready to kill me.

I hear her sniff. Little sniffs at first, then long, drawn-out sniffs. Outside my cubicle.

She can smell me.

I move my nose to beside my armpits and I'm not surprised. I haven't changed since the whole Mrs Hogsmith debacle. I've been sweating out of fear for most of the day, and I must be giving off quite the stink.

Kaylee, what should I do?

I don't ask aloud, but I ask anyway.

Am I pathetic? For needing my twin sister to calm my nerves? It's sad, maybe, but she has an uncanny ability to take my emotional baggage and condense it into its smallest, most insignificant form.

Funny, really. I'm travelling the country to save her, but honestly – what could I do if she is in trouble?

Then again, I would know for sure if she is alive and sane.

And I need to know.

Which means I need to deal with this woman outside the stalls.

I put my feet down. Take a deep breath. Ready myself for a fight.

And that is when I hear the others screaming.

CHAPTER TWENTY-SIX

Patrick and Clyde panic.

Which is expected of Clyde, as he's still young.

Patrick, however, who so far has been a boastful prick, would be expected to display a calm ruthlessness – but when moments of true fear are revealed, so is our true character.

The women surround them. Edging closer. They aren't running this time; they don't need to. They have formed a circle and their prey is in the middle of it.

Fight or flight kicks in. There is no fight. Not with this many of them. Patrick can swing his knife back and forth as much as he wants, one of them would still manage to get to him.

Then again, they cannot get out of the services the way they came as the exit is blocked – so they can hardly run; fight it is.

"Get a weapon," Patrick tells his son.

Clyde slides over the McDonalds counter and searches. The deep fryers are long since cooled, there is no machine that can easily be uprooted, and a few chicken nuggets are hardly much of a deterrent.

Then he notices the till screen. It is not attached. He picks it up and slides back over the counter.

Just as one of the bitches approaches Clyde, he lugs the screen forward, smacking it into her face and taking her to the ground.

A good solution, maybe, yes – but seeing as there are another seven or eight approaching, it doesn't do much in the grand scheme of things.

Patrick tries to think. Tries to stay calm, figure out what to do.

If he could lure them into a smaller space and create a funnel, one where they couldn't all come at him at the same time, then it would be easier to fight them off.

The bathroom! They could stand by the door and take them out one by one.

"This way," he tells Clyde, and he runs, his son following.

They pass the clothes, pass the games and slot machines where Patrick would normally split up long journeys by wasting his money, and past the newspaper stand he almost runs into.

He glances over his shoulder, which is a mistake. They are close, and they are running, and with every step he takes they gain another few.

He kicks open the door to the toilets and bursts in.

A woman, alone, wearing a short skirt over legs covered in a dried, red crust, stands in front of one of the cubicles, sniffing.

"Hold the door!" Patrick tells Clyde, who tries to push the door closed. The women barge against it and he struggles, and they both know he will be overpowered fairly quickly.

The bitch in the toilet notices Patrick, and runs at him.

He holds his hunter's knife at head height and the stupid woman runs straight into it, her eyeball squelching as the blade pierces it and sinks through to her brain.

She falls to the floor and he tries to take the knife out, but it's wedged into her face too much.

The door to the bathroom bursts open, and Clyde falls to the floor.

Just before Patrick can understand what's happened, the cubicle door behind him bursts open.

CHAPTER TWENTY-SEVEN

I RUSH OUT of the cubicle and straight into Patrick's fist.

I am about to declare him my saviour and thank him for killing the woman lurking around the bathroom, but he reacts instinctively and knocks me to the ground.

"Ow!" I say.

"Oh, it's you," Patrick replies.

Before we are able to say anything else, a load of rabid women burst through the door. Patrick lifts Clyde to his feet and sprints to the fire exit at the opposite end of the bathroom, Clyde behind him, and me following.

We race out of the bathroom with half a dozen women trailing us, their arms stretching, fingers clasping, desperate to catch us. As I glance over my shoulder, I realise that a few metres is the difference between survival and a violent, dismal death.

It isn't too far. The women may be quicker than us, but we just have to make it around the corner without being caught.

We can do it; I know we can.

Not that we are much of a 'we'– Patrick couldn't care less

if I died. In fact, it would probably be helpful, as it would distract our pursuers.

Still, they have the car, and I run, trying to keep up.

As I pass the bins, I push one over to create an obstacle for those behind us. A group of cars block the way and I skid over a bonnet, then leap over a dead body, trying not to look at the guy's mutilated face.

Aside from an obese woman in a McDonald's outfit that lags behind, our pursuers gain on us, and the half a dozen women soon becomes more. They lurk around the car park then, as we approach, their heads lift and they sniff, and with every few strides we seem to pick up another chaser. Empty faces become full of rage, silence becomes screams, and dormant bodies start sprinting with a sudden speed that contrasts so distinctly with the lingering emptiness they previously had.

It doesn't take long until there are easily twenty, nearly thirty.

But they don't stop there. More come, more rise to attention, more chase.

Within seconds there is a whole crowd of them, growling and moaning and snapping their jaws, and I wonder why they can't just leave us alone. We are humans, trying to go about our business without harassment – but you can hardly reason with these women, can you? I can hardly explain that we do not want any attention. They will chase us anyway; they will seek what they want and use us as pieces of meat.

The car comes into sight and we push ourselves just that little bit harder. I trail behind the other two, feeling the women gain on me, hear the footsteps, smell the body odour.

One of them reaches out for me and brushes my collar. I swipe her away, but it throws me off balance and don't try such a thing again.

I just focus on running, yet however much I run the

woman closest to me keeps trying to reach me and almost succeeds.

Patrick reaches the car and gets in. Clyde follows, getting into the passenger seat.

The engine switches on and, for a fleeting moment of dread, I think they are going to take off without me.

They start to move, slowly, loitering. Clyde opens the back door and I reach out for it, but one of them grabs me, and pulls me back, and I miss the chance. I swipe the woman's hands away and this throws her off balance, which gives me a few seconds to get away.

I gain on the car again, reaching out, and take hold of the door.

I climb onto the backseat and Patrick accelerates. I try to close the door, but one of them is clinging onto it with one hand, and reaching for me with the other.

"Kill it!" Patrick demands. "Kill it now!"

If I wasn't so damn terrified, I might retort with something like, "What do you think I'm trying to do?"

But, as it is, all I do is stare at this carnivorous woman as I sweat and fret and try not to be a wuss.

Problem is that I am a wuss, and this woman is managing to climb into the car and it is petrifying.

"Where's your knife?" I ask, thinking that would be pretty good right now.

"Not got it."

"What?"

At first, I think he just doesn't want to give his knife to me, then he adds, "Left it in the bitch in the bathroom."

I try to kick the woman away, but she grabs my foot. I kick back and forth, but she clings on pretty well.

Clyde leans over the seat and punches her in the face, twice, then three times.

This throws her a little bit, and gives me the opportunity to peel her fingers off my ankle.

Finally freed, I kick again, into her nose, feel a little guilty about it, and the woman flies onto the road, just as Patrick swings the car onto the motorway.

I hope she's okay. They can't help what they are doing. I know it's them or us, and it's ridiculous, but that woman has a family.

Even so, you can't help someone who isn't even able to understand what they are doing wrong.

"Fucking bitches," Patrick says. "All they are good for is fucking and shutting up, and now they can't do either."

I don't agree with him, but now is not the time for an argument.

Instead, I lie back on my seat, close my eyes, and wait for my breathing to subside.

"Oh, fuck," Patrick says.

I lean up. "What is it?"

He's staring at something on his dashboard.

I see what it is.

It's the petrol light.

We'd stopped to get petrol, didn't we?

"I didn't manage to fill the tank," he says. "We're going to run out."

As I make eye contact with Patrick in the rear-view mirror, he sums up with one word what I am sure represents the feelings of everyone in the car.

"Shit."

CHAPTER TWENTY-EIGHT

WE PASS a sign for the next services after ten minutes. It tells us it's thirty miles away.

The dashboard tells us we have ten miles of petrol left.

I bow my head and sigh. My phone tells me it's somewhere around midnight and, honestly, these things were terrifying enough in the light – I don't want to be stuck in a broken-down car in the dark, open for attack while you can't see them coming.

"It's fine," Patrick insists. "I'll get off at the next junction, hopefully there'll be a petrol station nearby."

But when the next sign comes, telling us that the next junction will be in twelve miles, we know we will not make it.

The best thing to do is to go slowly and make the petrol last longer. This logic doesn't seem to occur to Patrick, as he speeds up, like he's trying to outrun the flashing number on his dashboard.

I consider pointing out that this is far from the best idea, but let's be honest – would you tell an aggressive Scottish guy who already hates you that his plan isn't the best plan?

Maybe you would. If so, you're a confident person who is probably very successful in life.

I'm not.

So when the car chugs to a stop in the middle of the motorway, and Patrick lifts his fist back and launches it at the steering wheel with a loud "fucking cunt!" I consider it the best idea not to tell him that his plan was doomed to fail.

Instead, we sit in silence. In total darkness. Exposed and stuck. Ripe for the pickings.

I stare out the window. Looking for movement. Looking for a potential assailant.

They could come from anywhere.

There are numerous abandoned cars, many trees and bushes along the side of the motorway, and beyond that, more darkness.

I shake. I can't help it. I can't see anything, and one of them could come from anywhere. Hell, a whole horde of them could come from anywhere. I've been lucky too many times; maybe I won't make it to Edinburgh after all.

"We'll siphon petrol," Patrick says. "Clyde will keep watch in the car."

"What?" I reply.

"There are loads of cars around here. They must have petrol in. We take it."

Before I can object – as if I would – Patrick gets out of the car, walks to the boot, and collects two buckets.

"Get out," he says to me.

I really do not want to get out but, forever being a coward, I do as I'm told. He hands me a gas can and a tube, and it makes me wonder – does he steal petrol often?

He pauses by Clyde's window.

"You all right?" he asks.

Clyde nods, clearly on edge.

"This way," Patrick instructs me.

I follow him, looking around, even though I can't really see anything. I use the flashlight App on my iPhone, but it doesn't show me what's in the distance. There are no lampposts, no source of light, nothing – anything could creep up on us, and I really don't like it.

"Point your light at what I'm doing," Patrick says, stopping by a Nissan Micra. "And keep watch."

I point my light at the fuel cap. Patrick puts one end of the tube in the car, and the other in his mouth.

Jesus, is he going to suck the petrol out?

"What?" he grunts, seeing me stare at him as he wraps his lips around the shaft and sucks. It isn't long until he takes the tubing away from his lips and the petrol starts pouring into his bucket.

That's when I hear it. A screech. In the distance.

"Patrick…" I say.

The bushes shuffle.

A shadow flickers by a car.

Feet patter along the surface.

"Patrick…"

"What?"

I peer into the distance, but I see nothing.

"Patrick…"

"What is it for fuck's sake?"

"I – I don't think we're alone."

The screech repeats, this time louder, and far more definite.

Patrick abandons the gas can and sprints back toward the car. I follow, and as soon as we're back in, he locks the doors.

We stay still and silent for minutes, just listening, watching.

Nothing appears.

But we know what we heard.

Patrick looks over his shoulder at me. Says nothing, just

stares for a moment, as if hatching a plan and trying to decide what use I'd be to it.

Then he looks at Clyde, and notices the expression of discomfort on his son's face.

"We wait for morning," he decides. "When it's light, and we can see, we do it then."

He turns to look at me.

"We'll take it in turns keeping watch. You go first."

I nod.

"Think you can manage that?" he asks.

"I think so."

"If anything happens–"

"I'll wake you up, got it."

Patrick turns to his son.

"Try and get some sleep," he says.

Clyde closes his eyes, though I don't imagine he'll have a good night's sleep. I'm not sure any of us will.

I turn to check Kaylee is okay, and ask her if she thinks we'll be okay.

She's not there.

Why do I keep doing that?

EXCERPT FROM WHEN WOMEN
ATTACK PODCAST EPISODE 5
(TRANSCRIPT)

Tell us about your role.

You mean my job?

Yes, your job.

I am a motorway regulator. Well, I was. It was my responsibility to monitor the messages that display on the screens you drive past.

Like the ones that say don't drink or drive, or beware strong winds.

Yes, those ones.

Okay.

I also help with the smart motorways in regulating the speed limits. If a lane needs to be closed because of a stranded vehicle I organise the messages for that as well.

So any time we had a traffic jam...

(*Chuckles.*) Yes, that would be my fault.

Finally, someone to blame.

Yes, finally.

I imagine most listeners to the podcast would wonder why I chose to speak to you. I mean, so far, I've interviewed government medical advisors, police officers... but they may not realise that you actually had quite a significant role in this whole situation.

A role in recognising a red flag, I guess.

A red flag?

I saw on the cameras that the motorway was getting clogged up. It was like a drain with lots of hairs in it...

Nice analogy.

(*Laughs.*) Sorry, my wife's hair was constantly making the sink and the bath take ages to drain, and it often wound me up, so I guess I thought – well, that was how it was. More and more hairs – or, should I say, cars – kept going into the drain, the road, this – this – three-lane passageway. It wasn't long until there were so many cars that the motorway was too full, and it came to a complete stop.

What about the fields around the motorway? Surely it's not like a drain, because you're not–

Just going to stop you there. Those fields… Where do you think they came from? They weren't just waiting on the motorway, were they? They came from elsewhere.

Who?

The women. They could practically smell the testosterone, shoved together among hundreds of thousands of cars. It was like an all-you-can-eat buffet. And these cars… They weren't going anywhere. Meaning that these men, desperately trying to escape the cities or get to loved ones or doing whatever they thought they were doing, they were stuck … They were easy kills. It was like a deer putting itself in the most exposed place to be hunted, and standing still while the hunter pulled the trigger.

And, ultimately, I guess it worked to the women's advantage.

Worked to their advantage? There's an understatement. They came charging, sprinting across the field, like a swarm of locusts, smashing windows, pulling men out the cars… It happened within the first few hours. I watched the CCTV, trying to coordinate with the police, then the army, until they just gave up.

They gave up?

Would you go into the lion's den to take back its prey? No! You would damn well leave it alone.

So it was like a free-for-all?

EXCERPT FROM WHEN WOMEN ATTACK PODCAST EPISO...

Half a day, it took. Half a day until the entire motorway was done. So many cars had mounted the verge, tried getting away. I mean, with all the cars trying to drive into the fields to escape, the motorway did become clearer, but... Those people stood no chance. By the afternoon, the motorway was empty of life and full of bodies.

And that was the end of the motorway?

Not quite. See, these women seemed to have lost a bit of intelligence, and couldn't figure out how to open car doors. So while most smashed windows, ate, and left, some of them had forced their way into cars, and ended up trapped inside.

What did they do then?

Waited.

Waited?

They just waited. I watched them, lying down on the backseat, or sitting so still you wouldn't see them among the shadows. They just waited for some poor bastard to come along and find them.

Wow.

Yep. The motorway, even when empty of people, was still one of the most dangerous places to be.

CHAPTER TWENTY-NINE

Patrick snores like a rhino.

I don't know how he managed to get to sleep so easily, but he did, and he sounds like a warthog in mating season. Every exhale has another snort and a smack of the lips. It's disgusting.

I don't know if Clyde is asleep. He doesn't make any noise, but maybe he's just not a snorer.

I look out of the window, keeping watch, trying to stay focused. Honestly, I am tired. Very tired. It's been a trying day, and that's putting it mildly.

But I don't know if my mind would let me sleep.

After a few hours, a particularly embellished snore from Patrick seems to wake himself up. He looks around, alert, and turns to me.

"What is it?" he asks.

I shrug. "I didn't say anything."

Patrick checks the time.

"I'll take watch," he says. "You get some sleep."

I faintly nod. It's a few hours before morning, and I don't see myself being particularly restful. Still, I lie down, but I don't try closing my eyes. Instead, I stare at the ceiling of the car. It's usually grey, but at the moment it's black. Pretty much everything is, such is the weight of the darkness.

I sigh. Try and decide on what to think about. What fantasy I could indulge in that might rest my mind and allow me to sleep.

I imagine what I might say to Kaylee if I find her.

When I find her.

Will she be okay?

What will I do if she is not?

What if she tries to kill me?

What would I do if my best friend in the world is a murderous psycho hell-bent on feeding on me and tearing out my insides and...

Well, this isn't working. My mind is not restful. If anything, I'm more alert than I was when I lay down.

I open my eyes. Watch Patrick's head as it turns, back and forth, no doubt searching for potential attackers.

Is this what life is now? Survival? Being constantly on guard?

If I don't find Kaylee alive and intact, then what happens next? Where do I go? What is my purpose?

If I'm with Kaylee, then we can find somewhere together, barricade ourselves in, stock up on tinned food, maybe in a library where Kaylee can read books or in an attic somewhere where no predator will find us.

But on my own...

I don't have a large circle of friends. In fact, my social life is generally limited to Kaylee, the bookstore, and my family.

The bookstore... I hadn't even thought... I wonder if my colleagues are okay...

Even if the government is still intact and trying to stop whatever's happening, I doubt they would prioritise protecting a bookstore. It's unlikely that, come the end of the world, people are going to seek out a good read to escape from the terrors.

I sigh a big sigh. This isn't working. I'm not sleeping.

I give up, for now, and take my phone out, dimming the screen so the others won't know I'm on it. I try texting Kaylee again:

On my way to get you. Wherever you are, stay safe, and stay hidden. Won't be long now.

I send it, adding it to the list of other undelivered messages.

I turn the volume of the phone down so only I can hear it and ring her.

"Hi, this is Kaylee, I can't get to the phone right now but if you leave a message I will get back to you."

I hang up.

Ring her again.

Listen.

"Hi, this is Kaylee, I can't get to the phone right now but if you leave a message I will get back to you."

It's ridiculous, I know.

But it's like she's right next to me.

If I can hear her voice, then she's okay, right?

"Hi, this is Kaylee, I can't get to the phone right now but if you leave a message I will get back to you."

I stop. Let the phone drop from my hand. This isn't comfort, it's torture.

I close my eyes. Force myself to try to sleep.

I get half an hour, if that.

CHAPTER THIRTY

I WAKE up as the sun rises, and Patrick seems to have come up with a whole new plan.

"Fuck this car," he says, looking at his Citroen Grand C4 Space Tourer MPV with disgust. "I only bought it because the missus insisted on having something to take the kids around."

He surveys the selection of abandoned cars displayed before us, opening his arms grandly.

"Look at this. We could have anything now. BMW. Ferrari. Jaguar. We just need to find one with the keys still in. Bound to happen, people must have left their cars in a hurry. I don't have a wife to tell me I can't anymore."

He looks at me and grins.

"That cow dying is the best thing that ever happened to me. Nagging bitch."

"I take it you weren't married long."

"Twenty-six years. Met her in school. Big mistake. She went from being a stunner to a hackit bitch."

"Hackit?"

"Ugly."

"Ah."

It's amazing how, as soon as you cross the line from England to Scotland, it's like they are speaking a whole new language.

"Let's look for a wee car then. And don't get me one that's scabby."

"Scabby?"

"Dirty, for fuck's sake."

Shaking his head, Patrick traipses between the cars, looking in each one and checking for keys. Clyde follows behind, carrying bags.

I try to make it look like I'm doing the same by looking in the windows of various cars, but really, I am watching him.

Something about him is making me feel increasingly nervous. I mean, he has been a dick from the moment I met him, but now… it seems like there's an extra cocky edge to him.

Like he's getting more boastful. More arrogant.

More reckless.

"Yeah, getting married was the biggest mistake I ever made," he continues to rant as he scans the cars. "All they're ever good for is a quick shag and it's time to say goodbye. Let one stick around and you end up stuck with them, nagging you every moment. Should have struck that cunt down before this all happened. I was glad when she turned rabid, it meant I finally had an excuse."

I suddenly want a weapon.

I feel like I need one. Like I'm going to need to use it.

Not necessarily against the rabid women, but against Patrick.

His son ignores him. Maybe he's used to hearing this.

Honestly, I will never get used to it.

"Cheated on her six fucking times, too, you know. Six.

She never had a clue. One of them was with her best friend. Fucking stupid, she was."

I look into each car, but I'm not looking for keys.

I'm looking for a knife. Or a hammer. Or anything I can use.

I see something in a Volkswagen. It's long and large, with a curved blade. A machete, maybe. Covered with speckles of blood, but I can't be fussy.

I open the door and, just as I do, Patrick turns to look at me. He stares, wide-eyed, in that way that thick people do when expecting you to agree with their moronic statements.

I freeze. Terrified. Like I've just been caught.

I'm sure he won't know I'm reaching in to get the weapon, it's just the timing of it – he turns at the exact moment I place my hand into the car.

I feel suddenly stupid. A weapon? Really? I've never so much as punched a guy. How would I wield a machete?

"You ever married?" Patricks asks.

It stumps me. I wasn't expecting casual conversation.

"I, er… no."

"Good on you." He notices the car I'm reaching into. "Leave that one. I don't want no fucking Volkswagen. I want something good." He turns and swaggers forward. "A fast fucker, something that shows these bitches I am not to be fucked with!"

With his back turned, I reach in, and wrap my fingers around the handle. I do not take my eyes off him, watching his back as he saunters around with arrogant strides, each step full of conceit and self-assurance, and I slowly take the machete out, keeping it behind my back.

I tuck it down the back of my trousers, and put my t-shirt over it.

"These bitches ain't changed. This is how they've always

been. Feeding off us, taking what they want – it's only now they've stopped being discreet about it."

I walk toward him, slowly, still watching, still cautious.

He finds a BMW, opens it, and retrieves the keys. With a big smirk, he turns to me and says, "All of these whores deserve what they get for fucking us over since the dawn of time. I want to slay each one of these cunts, cut them open like they deserve – what about you, kid? Don't you?"

He stares at me.

He expects an answer.

Like it's a test.

Clyde stops and looks at me too.

I should say yes. I should just agree, give him the affirmation he wants. No one will hear, it's just a lie, purely for survival.

But, somehow, I feel Kaylee beside me. Her judgemental eyes. She's not there, but she's my twin, she'll know.

I hear every rant about sexism Kaylee's ever had.

Every complaint about the promotion she applied for where a man was offered the job over the other three female candidates.

Every observation on how books often describe men as shouting, but women as shrieking or screaming.

Every grievance about the unrealistic expectations of the media on the female body – how every cover of a women's magazine features a headline about how you should be comfortable with how you look, and another headline about which diet will help you get that killer body.

And I finally see Patrick for who he is.

He's the bloke at work who said she looked fit and was angry that she didn't just take it as a compliment.

He's the male boss who told her she should smile more as she isn't coming across as particularly appealing.

He's the man who catcalls her as he drives past in his van.

And, with Kaylee's voice echoing around my thoughts, I say the one word that would appease her, and might ultimately lead to my own downfall.

"No."

Then I follow it up with a more assured, and equally foolish, "I do not."

CHAPTER THIRTY-ONE

"What did you just say?"

"I – I, erm…"

"You what?"

"I just don't agree with how you talk about women, that's all."

What the hell am I doing?

Why is now the time I choose to be confident enough to speak my mind?

I've been a lemming all my life, why is it this particular moment when I choose to change?

"You doaty fucker," he says. "These bitches try and kill you and you're still on their side?"

"I think they need help."

"Help? They try and kill you and you want to help them?"

"They don't understand what they are doing is wrong. I mean, I'll defend myself when they attack, but generally–"

"Who the fuck are you? Some prissy middle-class twat, thinking you can condescend to me?"

"I'm not condescending, just disagreeing."

He shakes his head.

"Get the bags in the car," he tells his son, who puts the bags in the boot and gets in the BMW.

Patrick does not go to the car. Instead, he edges closer to me.

I put my hand behind my back and grip the machete, just in case I need it.

"I help you," he says, "out of the goodness of my heart. And you disrespect me?"

"I am not disre–"

"You think you're better than me?"

Honestly, I do. I think a cockroach is better than this guy.

Knowing that I am somehow incapable of lying at the present moment, I say nothing, and in a way, that's probably worse.

He steps toward me, his fists clenching, ready for a fight.

Without thinking, I take the machete out and point its tip toward him. He is metres away, and if he comes closer, I'm not entirely sure what I'll do, but hopefully the weapon is enough of a deterrent.

The look on his face is, at first, is one of abhorrence. Disgust that I dare do such a thing.

The next is laughter.

My arm is shaking. The machete is wobbling back and forth. I am sweating. I don't even know if I have the guts to use it.

I am bloody terrified of this guy. I didn't realise it, but I realise it now.

And he sniggers at me.

"You can walk to Scotland," he says, and charges toward the car.

Half grateful he hasn't kicked my arse, and half annoyed my ride to Edinburgh is disappearing, I don't move.

What the hell am I doing?

I can't even drive. It's not like I could nick one of these cars.

So I stand, still shaking, and watch as Patrick gets into the car and turns the ignition.

All three of them avoid looking back at me.

Wait.

What?

All *three*?

That's when I realise there is someone on the backseat. Someone who must have been lying down, and is now sitting up. I only see their silhouette, but this silhouette unmistakably has long hair and breasts.

Some guys have long hair and breasts, right?

Acting instinctively, I chase after them.

"Wait! Wait, you're not alone!"

The engine roars as the car begins to accelerate.

"There's a woman in the car!" I shout, but it's lost in the noise.

As Patrick speeds away, he sticks his middle finger out of the window.

"No, stop, there's a woman!"

I watch the car travel into the distance. After a few seconds, it swerves and crashes into another car.

Then it doesn't move.

I wait for Patrick to burst out of the door, or for the car to accelerate again, but it doesn't.

Five, ten minutes pass as I stand here, watching expectantly, and there is still nothing.

I go to the other side of the motorway, giving the car a wide berth as I pass it. As I do, I can see two silhouettes through the window, completely still, and another feeding on them.

I turn away from the car. Try not to look. I walk on,

checking the window of every vehicle I pass, until I am out of sight of the BMW Patrick tried to commandeer.

I look around. I'm completely exposed. If something runs out of a nearby field, or out of a car, I have nowhere to go.

I need to get to safety.

No – I need to get to Edinburgh.

But I have no way to get there.

I take out my phone. Use Google Maps to see how far it is.

Twenty miles.

Just twenty miles.

I've come so far…

A growl echoes in the distance.

I bow my head. Is this it? Is this as far as I can get?

Then something catches my attention. On top of a nearby car, fixed in place – a mountain bike.

I haven't ridden since I was fifteen and failed my Silver Cycling test, and twenty miles is a long way to cycle, especially for someone who has never exercised or even set foot in a gym; but I have no choice.

"Stop being a prick," I hear Kaylee tell me.

And she's right.

I climb onto the car and get the mountain bike.

CHAPTER THIRTY-TWO

I HAVE a cousin who's really into fitness. He does a lot of running, biking, and sometimes does marathons. He's always going on about his 10k, like I know what that means. He and his kid often go on bike rides, and they will cycle all the way from Cirencester to Cheltenham, drop in for a drink, then cycle back again. It's easily fifteen, twenty miles to mine, then the same back again. They show up in their biking gear, drink some OJ, then head back again without so much as a sweat.

I must say, I am NOTHING like my nephew.

According to the Google Maps App on my iPhone, I have cycled eight miles, and still have twelve to go.

It is killing me.

Firstly, never mind the fatigue, what is up with the seat on a bike? It quite literally kills my crotch. My scrotum is half perched upon it, half off. I've always wondered why cyclists wear such ridiculously tight shorts – maybe this is it. It is not a comfortable seat and, as well as the ache in my dick, my arse feels like I've been sitting on a cheese grater.

Secondly, ignore when I said never mind the fatigue. The

fatigue is the worst. I don't know how my cousin does that many miles and show up looking like it's nothing. My legs ache, and my arms ache, and my neck aches, and my nipples are somehow sore despite not being involved in the cycling.

I remind myself I may still have to battle my way through a hall of residence of psychotic women to get to Kaylee, and slow down a little to preserve energy. I really need to get to Kaylee, and quickly – but I'll be useless if I can barely stand.

I wonder if she knows I'm coming – in the same way that I know, deep down, that she is still alive, I wonder if she can feel that I'm on my way.

She probably thinks I'm being an idiot. Kaylee is the one who sticks up for me, who tells bullies to piss off, who makes sure I'm okay. If anyone was going to protect anyone, it would be her protecting me – chances are, once we're reunited, I'll just be a burden.

But I have to know.

I mean, I'm sure she's fine – but I have to see for myself.

A few decades ago, the government actually did some studies on twins, to see if there was genuine telepathy. They put twins in controlled conditions and did test after test. In the end, they could not conclude that they had evidence of any genuine telepathy.

Well, whatever their scrupulous experimentation may have suggested, I know what I know.

In fact, when we were kids, we often used to communicate without talking at all. We'd be at the tea table, eating our fish and chips, or roast dinner, or sausage casserole, or whatever Mum had made, and we'd look at each other, and we'd send messages.

Not anything hugely elaborate, just stuff like, *Dad smells.*

And the other would start giggling.

Dad would look at us and say, "What are you laughing at?"

"Nothing, Dad," would be the innocent reply.

I'd look at her and think, *Mum smells too.*

We'd both laugh, sneaking looks at Mum.

"What?" she'd say, exchanging a look with her equally clueless husband. "I don't understand, what is it?"

What about Shania? Is she smelly too?

"Quit it!" Shania would say as we gave her a glance as well.

They are all smelly but us.

So true.

And then we'd smile.

I'm glad you're my sister.

I'm glad you're my brother.

Of course, through adult eyes, I do harbour a bit of scepticism. I have no way to know that her reply was *I'm glad you're my brother* and that it wasn't just something I imagined her thinking. She may have just been giggling because I was giggling.

In a way, I can understand why this method wouldn't have much integrity in a controlled experiment. But, just in case, in the possibility that I am right, and she can hear me, I send her a message now.

I'm coming, Kaylee. Just hang on, I'll be there soon.

I cycle harder.

Only a few miles to go now.

With another surge of adrenaline, I fight through the ache in my legs until I'm nearly there.

It's beginning to get dark again when I approach Edinburgh. As I get closer to the city centre, there are more and more noises that make me worry, but I just keep going.

Until, eventually, I arrive at the Royal Mile. From here, it is just another mile until I arrive at Edinburgh University's hall of residence.

CHAPTER THIRTY-THREE

THE POLLOCK HALLS OF RESIDENCE has a stylistic mixture of the old and the new, with modern designs mixed with 19th century buildings. To my right is an old-fashioned building that looks more like a castle than student accommodation, and ahead of me is a contemporary building with white walls and brown brick. There is no sign of life anywhere, male or female. This should reassure me, but it doesn't – chances are that, if there are any women, they are hidden, around a corner or behind a door, lurking, dormant, waiting to catch a whiff of me, at which point they will spring to life and I will die at the final hurdle.

I cycle past the barrier, and stop at an empty taxi rank. I feel for the machete tucked down the back of my trousers. It's still there.

I need to stop overthinking everything. My task is simple. Find Kaylee's room, and stay alert.

Ahead of me is a small building with walls made out of glass and the words *Reception Centre* above the entrance. I creep to the cover of a few bushes, look around, then walk up to the building.

I peer in through the glass walls, but the darkness of late evening has arrived and there is no way I can make out what's hidden in the shadows.

I can't see anyone, but that doesn't mean there isn't anyone there.

I take a deep breath.

What the hell am I doing?

Am I really so stupid to think I can do this?

I'm going to get killed.

Then so what, I figure. This life will end up being pointless if I'm on my own, spending every day running from the opposite sex.

No, I need to do this.

Come on, Kevin. Stop being a chicken and do this.

Then again, people underestimate the advantages of being a chicken. It's actually quite an easy way to live. If you're too afraid to do anything then you'll find yourself never actually having to leave the house.

Stop it.

Come on.

Get a grip.

I creep forward, passing the bushes, and reach out to push the door open. My hand hovers as I see a streak of blood on the handle.

After taking a moment to gather myself, I press my shoulder against the door and walk in.

There is another set of double doors for me to go through. I peer through, but I can't see anything. No women, nothing.

But the darkness can conceal all kinds of terrors.

I stretch out my arm and open the door, slowly, and hold it ajar.

I wait.

"Hello?" I call out.

If something is there, surely it will come running at me, giving me a chance to shut the door and run.

Nothing reveals itself.

Which should make me feel more secure, but it does not.

I edge in, cautiously, slowly.

To my left is what used to be a waiting area. The chairs are upturned, the carpet is stained with blood, and the leaflet stand is shattered with its contents spread across the floor.

To my right, on a marble floor, is a long counter with computers.

I walk, as lightly as I can, to behind the counter.

I flinch at the sight of a dead man on the floor, his throat slit, his chest open. His blood has begun to crust and his body looks stiff.

He's been dead for a while.

Suppressing the urge to be sick, I pass him, scanning the screens for a computer that is still on. I find one, though it's covered in splatters of blood. Finding a box of tissues nearby, I clean it off, and sit on the edge of the chair.

I search the icons on the desktop and find a database. I open it and type in Kaylee's name.

I find it. She is in *Chancellor's Court*, which looks to be the building directly in front of reception. She is in room six on the third floor.

The third floor?

Will I have to fight my way through?

I stare at the building, considering how to get in.

There is a small tower-like section with glass walls around the staircase. I could climb up and smash my way straight into the third floor.

Bloody hell...

I never thought I'd come up with a plan that had the words *climb* or *smash* in it.

I'm going to need something to smash the window with,

so I scan the room, and take a piece of wood that used to be part of the leaflet stand.

I brace myself.

Time to be an idiot.

I march toward the first set of doors, open it, and go to open the exit.

Just as I do, the bloodied face of a demented beast with long hair stares back at me, her face inches away from mine with nothing but a pane of glass to separate us.

She wears a suit jacket with a name tag that says *I'm Joan Can I Help*, and grins like she's happy to see me.

CHAPTER THIRTY-FOUR

I AM STRICKEN WITH FEAR.

Rooted to the spot.

Motionless with terror.

Which is ridiculous, really – how many of these have I seen now? How many times have I come across psychotic women? How many times have I been chased?

Yet, with Joan leering at me, I still panic.

I'm on my own now. Dad won't help. Patrick won't help.

It's just me and the receptionist.

At first, I comfort myself that she's on the other side of a glass wall, therefore giving me protection. Then she takes a step back and charges at the door like a bull stampeding toward a target.

She pounds it with her head and leaves an imprint of blood, but it doesn't deter her. She charges again, taking a step back, driving forward and ramming her head into the glass, which shakes from the impact.

I know I don't have long until she manages to get inside.

What the hell do I do then?

Right, stop panicking. Just think. Come on, Kevin, think. What weapons do I have?

I have a machete, and a large piece of wood

Unfortunately, it is guts that I lack – which is probably the most necessary weapon of them all.

I look behind me. I could retreat. Go back in. Hide.

Then what?

Just wait for her to find me?

I look to my right. On the third floor of that building is Kaylee's room and, hopefully, Kaylee herself. Somehow, I have to find my way there.

But first I have to deal with Joan.

She pounds her skull against the glass, and each thump of her skull against the barrier between us makes me shudder.

Even though I know it's coming, it still makes me jump.

She rams again.

A crack appears.

She looks at the crack and – although I'm not sure whether this is in my head or actually in her facial expression – she seems to take great pleasure from the progress she's made.

I take out my machete in one hand. Hold the wood in the other.

No, this isn't going to work. I can't attack with both hands, I'll lose balance. I need both hands on one weapon so I can get what little strength I have behind it.

I opt for the wood. You may think I should go with the machete, but I feel I should save it. I need something that packs a larger impact when I swing it.

So I put the machete back down the back of my trousers. Hold the wood. Ignore the way it shakes as I grip it, and I wait.

Another pound against the glass and the crack grows larger.

I really don't want to hurt Joan.

Is that stupid?

I mean, she's going to try to kill me, and eat me, and maim me – yet I feel bad for any pain I may inflict whilst resisting.

She doesn't know any better. This is just how she is. She needs help, not repeated beatings with a large slab of wood. Yet, I think trying to talk rationally to her and educating her about the folly of her attacks against the opposite sex will do little to deter her from any violence she wishes to inflict on me.

It's self-defence. Right?

She pounds the glass again. The crack grows and a few little shards sprinkle onto the carpet.

My immediate thought is – *best not step on that barefoot*. Like when Kaylee breaks a glass in the kitchen. And it's pathetic, isn't it, how we always revert back to what we know?

I look at the building again. At the third floor.

Kaylee must be in there.

The thought gives me strength. Encourages me to persevere.

On the next strike, more shards of glass fall out and Joan is now able to fit a large portion of her head through the gap.

She stops taking the run up, and just strikes her head against the glass with the strength of her neck, her head matted with blood and full of glass, again and again.

I lift the wood.

I wish it would stop shaking, but my arms still quiver. My knees buckle. My entire body is pumping with adrenaline and my thoughts betray me with visions of what might happen.

Joan sinking her teeth into my neck and pulling out my Adam's apple.

Joan feeling nothing when I strike her with the wood and beating the shit out of me before I can react.

Joan opening my chest and eating my insides while I'm still alive and forced to watch.

Bloody hell, Joan, I wish you'd go away.

With another strike of her head she is in.

I change my mind. I drop the piece of wood and take out the machete.

CHAPTER THIRTY-FIVE

JOAN CLAMBERS through the gap in the glass and charges at me, her mouth open, her arms reaching for me.

I yelp, and it comes out in a little squeak.

She grabs hold of my throat and pushes me to the floor, easily managing to overpower me. That's the problem when your attacker is physically stronger – the fight is always so uneven.

As I land on my back, feeling slightly dizzy from my head hitting the floor, I point the machete upwards. She leaps on top of me and, as she does, my weapon slides through her belly; and I feel just awful.

Awful!

Poor Joan.

Her face curls up into a defiant snarl. I'm sure she's in pain, but all I see is aggression. Like my resistance has spurred her on.

She opens her mouth and tries to reach my throat but, alas, her stupidity prevails, and she just sinks further onto my weapon.

I try and slide out from underneath her but, even with her being impaled on top of me, she is too strong.

She lifts herself up, taking herself off the machete, onto her knees, and blood from the hole beneath her breasts gushes over me, turning my t-shirt and trousers completely red.

I mean, I wasn't trying to make a fashion statement, but I just look ridiculous now; and the sight of all this blood makes me gag.

I ignore it. Tell myself to stop being such a wimp. Push myself to my knees. Hold the machete back and thrust it forward, into her belly once again, retracting it almost as quickly.

I stand and back away from her.

Despite the continuous pool of blood gushing from her wounds, she still staggers toward me in a chaotic limp.

I'm going to need to deliver a fatal blow.

I know it.

But, again, I'm not Clint Eastwood or Bruce Willis or whoever your favourite action movie star is – I'm just a regular, timid boy who's never stood up for himself in his entire life.

She wobbles toward me. Reaching out. Her nails are long and sharp, and I think she's trying to slit my throat.

I close my eyes and scream as I swing the machete until something stops it.

I open my eyes and marvel at the sight of my weapon stuck in Joan's neck.

Her eyes widen and empty, then she falls to the floor.

I stare at her for a moment. I've struggled to look at the dead bodies I've seen in the past few days, and it's even worse to stare at one I've just created, and I know I'm going to be sick, so I run toward an artificial plant and throw up into the plant pot.

I haven't eaten much, and it is mostly blood and bile. Even so, another wave comes and I throw up again.

I lean against the wall. Not wanting to look at what I've done, but knowing I need to retrieve the weapon.

I cover my eyes with my hands so I can only see Joan's feet and edge toward her head. Without looking at the corpse, I reach out for the machete.

I can't find it.

How can I not find it?

Screw it. I uncover my eyes and look down at Joan's face, so still, so empty, and coated in blood. The machete sticks out of her throat, so I take hold of it and try to pull it out like that guy in *Sword in the Stone*.

Loads more blood fires out of her and sprays over my clothes. There's barely a part of me that is uncovered, and I look disgusting.

I huff. I'm just going to have to deal with it. At least I'm alive. At least I'm here.

I tuck the machete down the back of my trousers, pick up the slab of wood, and step out of the hole in the glass, walking toward *Chancellor's Court*.

Which is an incredibly stupid move as, in my desperation to get to Kaylee, I didn't check to see if the coast is clear; meaning I didn't see the group of five or six of them sitting over a body to my left, eating away.

By the time I notice them, they've already noticed me. Each of their heads lift and their demented eyes are focused in my direction.

"Shit…"

I turn and run toward the building. Between two solid walls is the staircase surrounded by glass walls. I leap onto a ledge, and onto the railing, and do so surprisingly well for someone who considers parkour to be the last thing I would ever consider taking up.

My legs dangle, and I almost slip. Their hands reach for my ankle.

I lift my legs up with great difficulty – I don't know if you've ever tried using a pull up bar in the gym, but it's difficult enough for those who actually work out. I just about manage to leave their outstretched arms and balance on top of the railing.

Without looking down, I pull myself up onto the next railing and perch on top of it.

Then I can't help it. I'm an idiot. I look down.

They are all there, waiting for me to fall.

Taking a deep breath, and trying to do this without thinking, I pull myself upwards and onto the next railing, which takes me to the third floor.

Holding onto the railing with one arm, and pressing my feet against the window, I use my spare arm to swing the wood against the glass.

The glass barely wobbles, so I try again. It takes ten or so strikes until I see the slightest crack, and I grow a strange appreciation for how quickly Joan managed to break through the glass door.

After more strikes than I can count, the glass finally begins to falter, and eventually smashes.

I climb in and fall on the floor, which is silly as the thousands of bits of glass cause many little cuts.

I stand. Brush myself off. Ignore the twinges of pain, and feel proud that I've made it this far.

I wait. Listening.

I can't hear anything, but that doesn't mean there's nothing there.

The door to rooms 1-8 is to my right. I open it slightly, and look into the corridor. There are only a few women, and they are all dormant. Just standing idly, shifting weight from one foot to another. I'm not fooled – as soon as they catch sight of me they will change to rabid monsters, and I have to be cautious.

On the right is room two, four, then six – Kaylee's room. I'm going to have to creep through. It's not too far. There are two doors then hers. I can try and go through the corridor unnoticed, and just hope that if one of them sees me I can get to the room before they catch me.

So I take a deep breath. Ignore my better judgement telling me this is ridiculous, and I enter the corridor on my hands and knees.

Surely they are less likely to see me if I'm on my hands and knees, right?

I crawl, slowly, making sure I do not brush past any legs without realising, staring at room six, focused on my destination.

I pass one of them and she starts sniffing.

Her eyes become alert and she looks around.

Another starts sniffing.

I pass room four. Just another metre or so…

They are all sniffing. All looking around.

One of them begins to turn, their eyes lowering, almost seeing me – so I do not waste any more time crawling.

I reach room six, Kaylee's room, and leap to my feet. I press down upon the door handle without looking back to see if any of them have seen me.

I enter the room and shut the door behind me, locking it as I do.

CHAPTER THIRTY-SIX

THE ROOM IS EMPTY.

There is a window to the darkness outside. A desk. A single bed left unmade – which is odd in itself, as Kaylee never leaves a bed unmade.

A phone is on the desk, plugged into the wall.

I approach it. I light up the screen and there are all the messages from me, unread and unanswered, along with all my missed calls.

Kaylee is like any other nineteen-year-old woman – she would not go anywhere without her phone. She doesn't update her social media much but is commenting on the nonsense other people post, and if you message her, she usually messages back within the hour.

This doesn't confirm anything, I know, but in a way, it does. It confirms that either she left in a hurry, or…

I hear a noise from behind me. I turn around quickly.

There is a door to the ensuite. I didn't realise this room had a toilet.

The noise comes again. Against the door. Every few

seconds. Like a banging without any rhythm – there is nothing but chaos to it.

Like someone is trying to get out.

I almost don't want to open the door.

Maybe the banging from the ensuite is coming from Kaylee's attacker. Whoever made her flee. Kaylee could have trapped her assailant in the toilet and ran. She could be hiding under the bed.

Despite my gut telling me she is not there, I look under the bed. Her rounders bat, her suitcase and a few empty boxes are there, but not Kaylee.

Slowly, I become resolved to what I don't want to admit – I am going to have to open that bathroom door.

The machete feels moist against my back, a mixture of my sweat and Joan's blood. I pull it out and clutch it in my right hand, then reach for the door with my left.

"Kaylee?" I try, just in case.

If it is her, then I want her to know it's okay.

"Kaylee, is that you?"

I wait.

Then I wait some more.

"Kaylee, this is Kevin, I made it here, I came to find you, just – if that's you, let me know you're okay, yeah?"

The door shakes as the bangs become more aggressive. Whatever's in there knows I'm here.

I take a deep breath.

Twist the door handle.

Prepare myself for the worst.

And open the door.

A rabid woman runs at me, placing her hands on my throat.

I panic, and drop the machete. Reacting on nothing but instinct, I take hold of the woman's throat and take her to the ground before she can choke me.

I place my knee on her chest and force all my weight on her, trying to pin her down. She is stronger, as they all seem to be, and she keeps shoving me off, but I return, forcing the entire mass of my body upon her.

Finally, I look upon her face.

It doesn't quite make sense at first.

My initial thought is… *Huh. How odd. This woman looks a lot like Kaylee.*

Then I realise it is Kaylee, growling and snapping, lashing out, and despite my eyes confirming it, I don't accept it. I just think, *Well, this doesn't quite make sense.*

I mean, I knew in my gut she hadn't changed. I knew. My twin intuition told me she was okay.

So I try to rationalise it. Think hard about what other explanations there could be.

The whole time, her arms flail, trying to get to me.

And I see her face again.

Paler. Sweaty. Matted hair. No blood on her mouth, but if she's been trapped in the bathroom she wouldn't have been able to hurt anyone.

Hurt anyone…

Kaylee? No, she couldn't…

But it is Kaylee. It's not an imposter, it is her, and that can only mean one thing:

I was wrong.

About everything, I was wrong.

My gut. My rationalising. My assurance that I knew…

It was all wrong.

She is just like the rest of them.

And I stare. Do nothing but stare.

She manages to shove me off, and she charges at me, trying to get to me, as if I'm no different to any other men, as if I'm just something to satisfy her hunger.

I back up, quickly, into the bathroom, and shut the door.

It rattles, shakes, and pounds.

She does everything she can to get in here but, just like the rest of them, is unable to understand what a door handle is for. It's like their intelligence has depleted and all that's left is this... angry mess. This thing that relies on instinct, that only thinks of themselves, that hurts what they want to hurt and doesn't care what trauma it leaves.

Meanwhile, I sink to the floor. Everything crashes around me. My life, my resilience, my perseverance...

This was all for nothing.

The whole journey here was pointless.

I have no family left.

I promised Dad I'd find her. And I did.

But I saw her, and I can't convince myself of anything but the truth. Not anymore.

Kaylee is one of them.

And I don't know what I'm fighting for anymore.

I give up.

Not just on Kaylee, but on life.

There is no purpose.

I'm left completely alone, with no reason to go on.

I bow my head. Let out a few tears.

It's over, I'm afraid.

It is completely, unequivocally, over.

CHAPTER THIRTY-SEVEN

I LEAN AGAINST THE DOOR, knowing she's on the other side.

Except, is she?

Is that Kaylee, or is it something else?

I'm not going to make far-out claims like this is some kind of oestrogen zombie apocalypse, but it does make me wonder how aware she actually is.

"Kaylee?" I say, like I'm asking a question.

She growls harder and launches herself against the door, just like the other women, she'd kill me if she could.

The next thing I know, I'm on my knees. I'm crying into my hands. I don't know how I got here, but this is where I am, and I do not know what is happening anymore.

Everything I was doing was for her. With this 50/50 chance that guy on the television claimed twins had.

And now...

Here I am. Inches away from her. But also inches away from being mauled and mutilated and eaten and killed and churned up and having my chest impaled and my intestines and guts and heart ripped out and...

I cry some more.

It's pathetic. I know I have to stop thinking about it. If I keep thinking I'm just going to feel worse and worse, but the only alternative is to cry, and I hate crying, Kaylee always took the piss out of me when I cried at films like *Titanic* or *The Perfect Storm* or during *The Lion King* when Mufasa dies and oh boy, if she could see me now.

The real Kaylee, that is. Not the monster on the other side of the door.

"Quit being a cry baby," she'd tell me.

"No one likes a bloke who bawls like a bitch," she'd say with a grin.

"You're never going to get laid if this is how you act," she'd claim with a playful nudge.

You're right, Kaylee. You're right. But what the hell am I supposed to do?

I thought you were alive.

I *knew* you were alive.

But you're barely here. Replaced by whatever it is you've been possessed by.

I stand. Wipe my tears.

Enough.

What would Kaylee do?

I ask this question of myself, not just fleetingly, but deeply and sincerely – what would Kaylee do?

Because, if this was the other way around, she wouldn't be on her knees crying by a toilet. She'd be doing something. She'd have a plan. Someway to get out of this.

But I do not want to get out of this without Kaylee.

She wouldn't abandon me, that's for sure. She'd do everything she could do to save me.

Even if I had no chance of being saved.

And, in this moment of realisation, I know what I must do.

I must not abandon her.

I must get her to safety.

I must get her out of this building, find somewhere to hide, and keep her safe until this all blows over.

I doubt there's a cure, or ever will be one, but what do I know? I highly doubted that all women would start killing and maiming men, so what we perceive as truth is not always necessarily that.

But how do I move her? How do I take her with me?

Think, Kevin.

What is there in this room?

What would Kaylee have that I can use?

She loves rounders. There is a rounders bat.

That's a start.

She can sew. She doesn't really do much, but she's always repairing torn dresses and t-shirts or whatever; she's always adamant she can salvage an unsalvageable item of clothing.

Which means she might have some string.

I sigh.

Damn, I'm actually doing this.

It's ridiculous.

I place my hand on the door handle.

I open the door.

Here goes…

CHAPTER THIRTY-EIGHT

I HOLD MY ARM OUT, grab her collar, and keep my arm straight.

She's strong, and it's hard to hold her off. Her hands clamber for me, her mouth chatters, opening and closing, her teeth chomping.

She's gone from being the woman every guy chases to the woman every guy runs from.

My eyes scan the room. I'm looking for the sewing kit, which must be in a box somewhere. And her rounders bat, that I know she wouldn't leave at home, not after how much she was looking forward to joining the rounder's society here.

I also took the mickey out of it. To me, rounders was always the sport you played in year seven when the PE teacher couldn't be bothered to think of anything better. But she loves it.

Well, she loved it.

Shit, should I talk about her in past or present tense?

My arm collapses; I've spent too much time deliberating, and I feel the heat of her breath on my cheek. I push her away with my other hand, straighten my arm again, and keep her at arm's length, trying to resist her strength – all while reminding myself to focus and stop thinking stupid, distracting thoughts.

She still has boxes on her desk.

The first one has CLOTHES written on it. I shove it out of the way. The next one has CLOTHES on it again. As does the next.

How many boxes of clothes do you have, Kaylee?

My arm almost collapses again, and I remind myself to focus.

I push the box out of the way, and the next has the words BITS ANDS BOBS on it. This must be the one. I open it with my spare hand and, sure enough, there is her sewing kit box. Inside of it is a load of string, and thick string too – strong enough that, if I wrap it around her enough times, hopefully it won't break. I take it out and place it in my pocket.

I look back at her. Her eyes are widening and she is still reaching for me and she always was so determined, so persistent.

I look around for the bat.

The bat, the bat, the bat…

It's under the bed. I remember when I was searching for her, and I looked under the bed – I saw it there.

I lower myself to the ground, watching her tower over me, until I am crouching, holding her at arm's distance, and suddenly gravity is helping her to be even stronger. The mass of her body is falling onto my arm and I'm not sure how long I can stand it.

I reach my other arm under the bed. Feel around. There's something fluffy but, under the circumstances, I ignore it and try not to recoil. Then I feel something hard and wooden, and I'm pretty sure that's it.

Just as my fingers meet the bat, my other arm collapses and her strength is too much.

In a swift motion, I pull the rounder's bat from under the bed and upper cut her chin with it, sending her onto her back, and I'm sure I see a tooth fly out of her mouth.

"Oh-my-god-I'm-so-sorry!" I say as I stand, clutching the bat, in shock at what I've just done.

She is not deterred. She clambers to her knees, and to her feet, and tries to get to me again.

I take the string and I let her get close, let her reach out for me, placing a hand over her throat as she gets closer, until she is inches from my face, and I can reach around her neck with the string, keeping it fairly loose so it doesn't suffocate her, but strong enough that she cannot wriggle out of it.

I tie the end of the string around the end of the rounder's bat, then around the rounder's bat again, then around her throat and around the bat until she's fixed in place and has no way of escaping.

I stand back. Holding the end of the bat and stretching my arm out so she cannot get to me.

I can move her around by moving the rounder's bat. I can keep her far enough away from me that her outstretched hands cannot reach my face.

Sighing, I look at her. My twin sister with her bloodshot eyes, fully dilated pupils, and I try to see if there is any of Kaylee still in there. If there is that compassion, that fire, that person who would take the piss out of me at every opportunity.

I'd like to pretend that I still see her in there, but I don't.

I don't see anything but an animal. Something desperate to kill me.

But that doesn't mean I'm going to abandon her.

Once I get her out of this building, then…

God, I don't know. We can find somewhere with enough

food and water to sustain us. Somewhere we can hide out. A supermarket, maybe.

Either way, there is no food or water in this room. We can't stay. We'll die. We have to leave, and we have to do it while I still have energy to fight – however weak I am at fighting.

I walk to the door, bringing her with me like a dog on a lead; or a sister on a rounder's bat.

I twist the door handle. Open it slightly. Peer out.

A few women still lurk in the corridor. I'm not going to be able to creep past them with Kaylee writhing and growling next to me, but if I can somehow find a way past them and down the stairs, then we can find somewhere to go, somewhere to see this out.

I look back at Kaylee.

Try again to see my sister.

All I see is a violent, feral creature.

What am I even doing?

Nope – no time to doubt myself now. Only time to get on with it.

I withdraw my machete, barge the door open, and enter the corridor.

EXCERPT FROM WHEN WOMEN
ATTACK PODCAST EPISODE 6
(TRANSCRIPT)

So you worked at Edinburgh University.

I was the dean, yes.

Were you the dean at the time of this happening?

No, I had retired, but I was still very close to operations at the university.

And you believe Edinburgh was, for lack of a better way to put it – Ground Zero.

For lack of a better way to put it, yes, I guess you could say that.

Why do you believe this?

Because reports came in here first. It was fresher's week at the time, which was the first few days that the first years arrived. Normally the student union provides night after

EXCERPT FROM WHEN WOMEN ATTACK PODCAST EPISO...

night of drinking and, well, young people becoming acquainted, shall we say.

Sex?

If you are to be so crude, yes.

And how was this fresher's week different to you?

Well, it's hard to quite put into words, but... Well... Normally, it's the men who are quite, well, er, predatory, shall we say. The new boys like to show off and puff out their chests and try to have relations with whatever young lady will relent. We try to have people on campus to educate women about keeping their drinks covered, about sexual health, about avoiding sexual assaults, but, well...

What?

In that first night, erm, well, the men were not the predators. In fact, we had reports by more than sixty male students that their drinks were spiked.

Spiked?

Yes. They were terrified. Then reports of student males not returning to their dormitories surfaced, and when they were reported missing and we went to find them in the rooms of whichever young lady their friends had seen them with, well... There wasn't much left.

How did this coincide with how everything happened with the rest of the country?

I believe Edinburgh's women started killing the men, maybe, the night before the rest of the country. I don't know whether it spread, or we were just unfortunate enough to have it first – but, what I can say, we undoubtedly had it the most horrific.

Yes, I heard about this. That the halls of residence were overrun before the news even caught wind of what was happening.

Yes, quite right. No man survived, and many, many women were left trapped in the halls of residence, hungry, waiting for the next man they could devour.

So the campus was swarming with them?

Oh dear boy, not even the army would go in there. They said it was pointless. They said everyone was dead and that it was best to leave the killers trapped in there.

So all the killers, the women, who had moved into halls of residence that week, were left in there?

Yes.

How many?

Every. Single. One.

CHAPTER THIRTY-NINE

THERE ARE FAR MORE women in this corridor than there were before.

The women that were here when I arrived had started sniffing, as if they could smell me... does that mean the rest of them can smell me?

Does that mean *all of them* are now heading in this direction?

If so, then this part of the halls of residence could become overrun very soon.

"Damn," I mutter, I wonder whether I should go back into Kaylee's room, but I close the door to stop myself. If we stay, we will starve to death – so I need to at least try to escape before even more come.

I need to have courage, like Kaylee would.

As I drag her into the corridor, I see more women in the way of the exit. The women behind me are absentmindedly hovering, dormant, like they are waiting, but as soon as they see me they become alert, pounce into life, ready for the kill.

"Shit," I say, but it's too late to back out now.

I grip the rounder's bat in my left hand, trying to keep

Kaylee too far enough away that her outstretched arms can't reach me, and I swing the machete back and forth, blindly, with no aim, just waving my arm and hoping to catch them.

Fortunately, these women aren't too intelligent, and a machete swinging through the air doesn't deter them. The first approaches and I catch her in the mouth; her jaw hangs for a few seconds by a stretched bit of skin, then falls to the floor. She isn't bothered – she just still reaches for me, with only the top set of teeth to bite me with.

I retch. Well, I almost do – I try not to. I have to focus. Have to deal with the violence I am about to not only witness, but commit.

Still, as determined as I am, her bottom set of teeth are just next to my foot.

Feeling a little disgusted, I kick it away, and keep swinging the machete at them, aiming it a bit lower; hoping to catch them in the neck rather than the mouth. The machete swipes through the throat of the jawless woman and she falls to her knees, blood spraying in a neat, curved line against the wall.

That's one. The corridor is narrow enough that they struggle to all get to me at once, but it's only a matter of time.

There are four more coming at me from the dead end of the corridor. I consider leaving them and trying to fight my way through the women blocking the exit, but they would just get to me from behind – I have to do something.

"Sorry, Kaylee," I say, and I put her between me and the women, using her as a shield. I swing the machete, back and forth, again and again, cutting a cheek, a shoulder, a chin, even a boob – but the fear that grips my shaking arm is affecting what should be an easy aim.

I steady it. Not well, but I do all I can, and I thrust into the next woman's throat, then pull the machete out. It's easier than I thought it would be – it slices in and out like butter. Another tries to reach for me and I cut her throat too.

The fourth and final woman from this side of the corridor lurches forward and, instead of reaching for my throat, she reaches for my bollocks, taking them in her hand and squeezing tight, tighter, and tighter still. She begins to pull and, in fear of losing what I treasure the most, I push the machete into her gut, pull it out, then lodge it into the side of her throat, allowing her to slide off it and onto the floor.

I turn, keeping Kaylee between me and the women blocking the exit, and I back up into the corner of the corridor.

This may seem like a bad idea, sticking myself into a dead end with nowhere to go – but in truth, this was the best thing I could have done. I am squashed against the corner, with Kaylee still reaching out to me, but there is only one direction they can come from now – straight ahead. Not from the side, or behind, and this means they can only come at me one at a time – meaning I can take them out one by one.

I lunge the machete into the eyeball of the first that approaches, then take the machete out and the woman falls to my feet.

The rest try to get past Kaylee, reaching for me, forcing my sister forward, and I have no choice but to bend my elbow and allow the rounders bat, and Kaylee, to get a little closer to me. She widens her mouth, reaching for my throat, and she is inches away, and I just have to let her stay there while I dispose of the women pushing her against me.

I can't get a decent swing of my arm, not with how hard I'm being shoved against the wall, so I lift the machete into the air and swipe down instead, landing it into the side of the neck of the next woman.

She falls, landing on top of the one with the eye-ache,

meaning the next woman stumbles over them a little bit, making it easier for me to plunge the knife downwards, into her neck. The next stumbles over three bodies, meaning it's easier to stab her as she falls. It gets even easier with the next one after that, and the next one after that.

With just a few remaining, I look at the pile of bodies, and I can't help but think – *I created that*.

Are they infected, or are they beyond help? Could they have been helped if I hadn't had to kill them?

I hope it's the latter. Despite what this would mean for humanity, I hope they are beyond hope – then I would not have to worry about what I've just done.

They were coming at me. It was self-defence.

I had no choice.

With my conscience screaming at me, I defy it and cut the throat of the next one, then the penultimate one, then, as I look into the final woman and say, "I'm sorry," I slice her neck and watch her fall to the floor.

It is just now when I realise that Kaylee seems to have lessened her attempts to get to my throat. She is watching me, her arms still reaching out, but more feebly, stroking me rather than grabbing, and I stare back, and for a moment, just for a moment – I see her.

I see Kaylee.

Not the cannibalistic murderer she has become. I see her. In there, somewhere.

And this only makes me more determined.

But it also makes me question what it is I see. I mean, I was so sure that I would find Kaylee still... well, like Kaylee. My twin intuition told me she was still okay. And it was wrong.

But these thoughts can wait.

I pull my legs from under the wayward arms of the

bodies, step over their backs, clutching the rounder's bat, and traipse through the corridor.

I pause as I see my reflection in the window to the kitchen. I know I'm covered in blood, but I hadn't actually seen what I look like. It's like I've just had a shower beneath a set of open veins.

I hold my breath, stare at myself for a moment, then move on, hoping I do not come across another reflection.

I open the door to the stairwell.

I thought having to fight the dozen or so that were in the corridor was tough.

That was nothing.

Because, standing there, at the top step of floor three, is far more than a dozen.

There are loads of them.

And I am not going to be able to fight them all.

CHAPTER FORTY

ALL I CAN DO IS RUN.

They fill the stairs, both up and down, but if I keep Kaylee between me and them, maybe I can barge my way through.

But they are so strong. Too strong.

Screw it, it's my only chance.

I run forward, dragging Kaylee, barging Kaylee into the first few women, and keep behind her, keeping to the side of the stairs, knocking them out of the way. My machete is in the other hand, and I manage to stick it into a neck or two as some manage to get past Kaylee.

But more are arriving. The crowd turns into a horde.

I can't do this.

Then I look back. The hole I made in the glass to get in here is still there.

It's a three-floor drop.

But it's the only way.

I drag Kaylee with me, keeping my head down. I don't even bother swiping my machete at them, I just cover my head, ensuring they can't get to my neck. I feel teeth on my forearm but I persevere, using Kaylee as my shield, and I make it back into the corridor and to the gap in the window.

There is a bush beneath us.

I don't hesitate. For the first time in this godforsaken battle, I don't hesitate. I just close my eyes and fall out, taking Kaylee with me, and, as we fall, I somehow feel Kaylee's arms around me.

For a moment, I wait for her to bite my neck, but she doesn't. She just holds me.

When I open my eyes again, she is below me, in the bush, and I quickly leap away from her before she can bite me.

But she doesn't try. Her teeth still chatter together. She is still pale, hungry, with a permanent snarl on her face. I remind myself that I still need to keep her at arm's length, even though she has stopped reaching for me.

I don't have much time to think. The women notice where I came out of and, one by one, they all start falling out after me.

I back up, dragging Kaylee with me, watching as they leap with no worry for the damage it will do.

Some of them get injured. One lands on her leg, it bends backwards, and she writhes on the floor. One lands on her neck and breaks it. Another lands on her face and, when she looks up, she has no teeth and her nose is broken to the side; even so, this doesn't deter her, and she gets up and comes after me.

Most only have a bruise or a cut for their troubles, and they climb to their feet and run after us.

I turn and sprint away from them, dragging Kaylee with me. Without a thought to what I'm doing, I aim for the admin building I was in earlier, trying not to look over my shoulder. I can hear the stampede of footsteps behind me, I don't need to see them.

I climb through the broken glass that Joan smashed her

head through, dragging Kaylee over it with me. She cuts her knee on a loose shard, but it doesn't bother her.

Hoping that these women still can't figure out how to open doors, I open the next door and shut it behind me, backing up into the centre of the small glass building.

And I watch helplessly as they surround the building.

Maybe a hundred. Probably more.

They charge at the building, each and every one of them trying to break the glass, just like Joan did.

This was a very bad idea.

Joan managed to get in with a few smashes of her head. Now I'm stuck, with women charging at the glass with their heads, their fists, and their bodies.

The window won't take long to give way.

It's just a matter of time now.

I look at Kaylee, who looks back, twisting her head, like she's eyeing up a nice, juicy steak, and I figure – if anyone is going to be the one to kill and eat me, I would rather it be her.

It's strange, really, how quickly I become resolved to death. I was fighting so vigorously, and now I realise it's over, and I accept it quickly. There is no more fight. To try and make it out of this alive would be futile.

I hear a smash. A crack.

It's minutes now, if that.

Minutes until they get in.

I untie the string from around Kaylee's neck. I drop the rounders bat. And I stand, looking at her.

She looks back.

"I'm sorry," I tell her. "Sorry I was wrong. That I couldn't save you."

I try not to cry. I do not succeed.

"I always thought you'd be the one who would end up saving me."

More smashes. More cracks. I see an arm reach inside.

"Please, just hurry up and do it, before they do."

She seems to understand me.

She edges forward. Places her left hand on my face. At first, I think it's an affectionate gesture, but it's not – she takes a clump of my hair in her fist, and I realise she is just keeping me still.

She pulls my head to the side, exposing my neck.

She stares at it.

I haven't seen one of these take so long, and I wish she'd hurry up.

The glass smashes completely. They are in.

I try to keep my focus on Kaylee, but I still see them flood inside over her shoulder, pushing each other out of the way, desperate to get to me.

Kaylee drags me to the desk, and pushes me to the floor so I'm by her feet.

She reaches for me, and this is it, this is it right now, and I get ready, ready for the pain...

But she doesn't bite me.

Her arm reaches past me, grabs hold of the machete, and pulls it out from the back of my trousers.

CHAPTER FORTY-ONE

She holds the machete, yet she doesn't use it against me, and there is a moment – a very small one, it lasts no more than a second, though it feels far longer – where she looks at me.

And I look at her.

And she's no longer the monster. No longer the creature.

But she isn't Kaylee either.

She's a child. Scared. Alone. Worried for both me and herself. Worried that we can't protect ourselves from this nasty world.

Then she turns and sticks the machete into the cheek of an approaching woman.

Shock would be an understatement. I am dumbfounded. But, Kaylee being Kaylee, she doesn't falter. She pulls the machete out of the woman's cheek and sticks it in the gut of the next one, then slices the throat of another, then another.

But there are too many of them. She can't fight the horde by herself, and God knows I'm of no use.

Still, she is not deterred. She moves in front of me, blocking me from my attackers, and I sit behind her legs like they were prison bars as she furiously hacks away at the oncoming women.

I'm six again. She's protecting me from the school bully. Or I'm seven and I've dropped my bag of sweets and she's offered me hers. Or I'm fifteen and she teases me for being a wimp than tells anyone else who calls me a wimp to fuck off.

But really, I'm nineteen. Stuck in this room with my sister fighting to the death to ensure my survival.

And I realise – nothing has changed.

We're still the same people. Whether baby, child or adult, the dynamic stays the same. I am on the floor like a coward, and she is standing up for me.

I was right.

My twin intuition was right.

She may have had symptoms; she may have even initially succumbed – but she hasn't changed.

She's still Kaylee.

And she's waving the machete back and forth, hitting whatever she can, using whatever strength or power she has gained through her morbid transformation, and she slices some of the women, wounds or kills another few, until the women stop advancing.

They don't back away, but they don't attack. I don't know how she's done this, or why these women don't realise how greatly they outnumber us, but they stop nonetheless.

They look at me, then look at Kaylee, snarling, waiting for a moment to strike.

But somehow, Kaylee keeps them all away.

Then she drops the machete by her side, and a sting of fear grips me and I think she's changed her mind, then she opens her mouth and lets out a huge roar.

It is partially a scream, partially a groan, partially a growl. It is a noise as inhuman as a human can produce, but I can tell what it means. It's something like *stay the fuck away* or *this one is mine* or *come near me and I'll gut you.*

The women linger, glaring at her, like they want to disobey her, but she is commanding too much authority over them, and no one is willing the stand up to her.

They don't back away, but they don't advance either.

She makes the sound again. Like she's telling them that she's the alpha woman – and no one messes with the alpha woman. The alpha woman is in charge, and the other women follow them like lemmings.

I have a fleeting feeling of hope, mixed with desperation. Kaylee curls her lip and leans toward them, showing them her angry stare, and it's so animalistic I half expect David Attenborough to start narrating it.

None of them defy her.

That is, until one of them does. A single woman breaks rank, leaps forward, and Kaylee grabs her by the throat and bites into their neck, dropping the body to her feet.

And she looks around at all the other women. Showing them what she's done. Showing what will happen should they attack.

And I wonder how long it will take for them to figure out that, however intimidating this alpha female is, if they all stood up to her, we'd have no chance. There are so many of them that, should they see a break in her confidence, they could take her down.

But they've just seen what she'll do to anyone who tries it.

Either way, the longer we stay here, the more likely we are to die.

We need to get out.

Now.

CHAPTER FORTY-TWO

Kaylee reaches behind herself, grabbing onto me, taking my shirt in her fist, and pulls me to my feet. She keeps her grip on me as I stand, and she begins to drag me toward the door, staring down all the other women as she does.

We edge along the desk, and the women back away. A few women are reluctant to move so she grunts at them, and they slowly and grudgingly move.

I want to ask her how she's doing this, but that may compromise her ability to do it. So I stay quiet. Not wanting to make eye contact with anyone, but unable to avoid looking at the angry but intimidated faces glaring at me.

We reach the end of the desk, and there are still so many between us and the exit.

She barks at them.

They don't move. They curl their lips defiantly.

Kaylee raises her eyebrows. A warning. An expression that says *just try it*.

A few of them move, but some others stay, trying to act confidently, trying to make out that they will not be coerced.

All Kaylee has to do is flex her fingers around the handle of the machete, and they finally relent.

She drags me to the door, pulls me through, and speeds up as we leave the building.

I look over my shoulder to see if they are following, but we turn the corner too quickly. Kaylee runs, dragging me with her as she does, her hand clutching my shirt, constantly scanning back and forth, checking it is safe.

It isn't long until we are out of sight of the halls of residence and on the Royal Mile – the main high street of Edinburgh.

Kaylee stops, still grabbing onto me, and looks around. She even sniffs. She's goes to walk, then stops us again, sniffing, like she can smell something but isn't quite sure.

She seems to decide it's safe and pulls me onto the high street.

We pass a few ransacked shops and a burnt-out cafe. It's strange, really – last time I was in Edinburgh was six years ago, when we came up to see some shows at the Edinburgh Fringe Festival. This street at the time was buzzing, full of street performers and people handing out leaflets for their shows. I was wearing shorts and sunglasses, and the crowds were so large you could barely move.

Now it looks like a desolate, dystopian street of death, marked with blood and silence. I'm not sure this city will ever see another fringe festival again.

There is a pub where the pedestrian part of the high street ends and the road curves past, about hundred yards or so before the castle. It's old-fashioned and its name has been destroyed, but it seems to be good enough for Kaylee. She pulls me down a side alley, and through the door to the pub, which she barges open.

It is dark inside, with old-fashioned wooden tables and very few windows, but it's unlikely we'll be found here.

Kaylee sniffs, and listens, and finally lets go of my shirt.

She turns and looks at me.

There is a vulnerability in her face I'm not used to, and a slump in her posture I've never seen.

I know immediately what she's about to ask me to do.

CHAPTER FORTY-THREE

THERE IS a sadness in her eyes. A look of resolve, of pain. A hatred of what she has become.

She looks down at her hands, dripping with blood. At the red hand prints she's left on my skin.

She falls to her knees.

I can see she's trying to cry, but she can't. It's no longer in her nature. It's not a part of who she is anymore, it isn't in her capabilities.

She is not one of them, but she's not quite human either. Stuck somewhere in between. A messed-up hybrid.

And all I can see is pain.

I fall to my knees with her. I take her bloody hands in mine, showing that I do not care what she's done.

Her eyes look at my neck. They linger, staring, and I can see she's trying to fight it, but she's hungry.

She's stopping herself now, but for how long?

It's probably been days since she fed and I'm surprised she's had this much energy, considering – but her movements are becoming slow and weary, fatigue is setting in, and I don't know how long she can fight what she's become.

She doesn't want to kill me, but a killer is what she is now. How do you stop yourself from becoming what fate has determined you will be?

"It's okay," I tell her. "It's okay."

She shakes her head furiously. She doesn't seem able to speak, but she understands me.

"You saved me," I tell her. "You saved me, and now I'm okay. I came back for you, and you saved me, and now it's all okay. We'll be okay."

We won't be okay.

Because I know what she wants me to do.

And I am not sure I'm able to do it.

She bows her head. Covers her face. I pull her arms away and she looks up, glancing at my throat again. A trail of saliva slithers from her bottom lip to her chin.

She holds the machete out and presents it to me.

I have no idea where it came from, or where she'd been carrying it, but she has it now, and she hands it to me.

"No," I tell her, but I know that she'll win the argument.

She wins every argument.

"Kaylee, come on."

Her lip curls and her impatience is evident.

I take the machete, but I hold it on my lap, loosely.

She leans her head to the side and exposes her neck, watching me with that same expression she had when we were nine and I stole her Tamagotchi and wouldn't give it back. It's a face of authority. A face that knows she will end up winning.

"Please, don't make me–"

She snarls. A grunt of wrath.

She is salivating again. Staring at my neck. Begging me to do it.

"I can't."

But I must.

I wouldn't want to live like this either.

But we could still make it okay. She could wear a muzzle, or keep away from me, and we could find a house somewhere and put things in place so I'm safe, make it okay.

But she would always need to feed.

People would always need to die to keep her alive.

She cannot help but succumb to her impulses.

I stand.

I ready the machete.

I have to do this for her.

I have to.

I hold it up.

Plunge it down.

And stop just as the tip reaches her skin.

She is furious. She snarls at me, growls, scrunches up her face in warning that if I don't do it soon, she'll do it to me.

But I just need to say goodbye.

I fall back to my knees. Put my arms around her. Hold her tight, squeeze her. Feel her breath on my neck, and I know what she's trying not to do.

So I pull back.

If she could cry she'd be bawling. I see it in her face, that desperation, the need for me to be strong.

So I hold the machete up in the air with both hands.

"Please don't make me do—"

She snarls again.

And again.

And she keeps snarling and snarling and growling and scolding me until I finally plunge the machete down into her neck her neck oh god it's in her neck I just did it I did it I…

I take the machete out.

Her blood sprays over the table. Over the bar. Over me.

She falls to her side.

Her eyes are still open. She is dying, but she is not dead yet. She is suffering, but it will soon be over.

So I pull her close, place her head on my lap, and stroke her hair.

She chokes. Splutters. Blood dribbles onto my already bloodstained trousers.

She looks up at me. Her vulnerability mixes with her love.

And her eyes empty.

It is done.

She is gone.

And I cry. Screw manliness, I cry. I cry like hell, cry my eyes out, cry until I have no tears left in me.

This is a shit world.

A fucking shit world.

And I hate it.

I HATE IT.

I look down at her. She stares upwards, like she's petrified, and I place my hand on her eyes and close her eyelids.

I lift her onto the floor. Gently, as if it matters.

And I stay with her until dawn arrives.

The pub remains dark, but out of a far window I see a blue sky, and I know the sun has risen.

I want to take her with me. To bury her. Give her a proper goodbye. Somewhere I can visit.

But there's no way I can get her body safely out of here.

So I leave.

Alone.

Into a world that causes nothing but fear to my gender. A world where a man isn't safe to walk home alone, never knowing what the opposite sex might do.

CHAPTER FORTY-FOUR

WHAT'S LEFT of the army finally gains some sense of control.

They have little they can do against the mass of women that outnumber them, but they at least manage to create a sanctuary. In fact, they create a few – twenty-six, to be precise. Small villages surrounded by large walls. Spread across the country, so all survivors will have somewhere to go.

A new government is assembled. I have no interest in voting or knowing who it is. It hardly matters – they can't change anything. But they do consider what to do with the women, and there is a debate with heated opposition on all sides.

Some say we should try and reintegrate them. Which is a ridiculous idea; as much as you try to alter their behaviour, try and show them how they should act, they still insist on acting as nature intends them to. Predatory and vile.

Some say we should quarantine them while we try and find a cure, whilst some say that there is no cure as there is no sign of infection. Some scientists claim this is something inherent in the nature of their gender, and it's something we can't change – whilst some say that we have to at least try.

And, of course, some say we should just wipe them out. This is dismissed as a last resort, considering it could put an end to our species – after all, it's not possible to reproduce without both sexes.

Which poses another debate – how do we reproduce with women as they are?

Then again, is the human race worth continuing, considering that one could give birth to a girl who would just go on to treat men like they are nothing but food, here for their consumption.

Whilst all of this is happening, I think a lot about Kaylee, and what happened, and one day I manage to seek an audience with the government. I tell them my story in hope that this will highlight the possibilities of the twin gene, suggesting that, should they find women who are twins, there might be a possibility that they could be saved.

I insist that there is hope that, despite the majority being unwilling to change, a few women could relearn some humanity.

I have no idea whether they take my suggestion on board, but I leave the room, knowing that I did what I had to do. That I shared my experience, and educated them as best as I can.

It is up to them if they do anything with it.

Meanwhile, I am given a room, and food, and live a safe life, away from the dangers of women. But I do often lie awake at night, wondering what will become of the world.

We now live in a society where its unsafe for men to leave their homes. If we were to leave our sanctuary, at worst we risk being abused or killed, and at best, we risk being taunted and made to feel dirty and unsafe.

Imagine such a world. It's horrific.

Of course, I can't just lie around in my room all day. We are told that we have to find a role. As in any society, we need to do a job, and contribute in some way.

I think carefully about what I could do.

I could help grow crops. Help with the farming. Each community has developed resources to grow food and it is essential that we have skilled men working on them. But I've never been much good at manual labour.

I could be a courier. Help transport goods between the sanctuaries. But I am not much of a fighter should something go wrong while I'm travelling from one place to the next.

I could become a teacher. Help young boys become strong, independent men. But I never did like school.

In the end, I help to educate in other ways. To provide the population with entertainment and reflection.

I create a podcast.

One where we share stories of what we've been through, and how we've overcome the abuse that women have forced us to suffer. I'm sure that our abusers would scoff at it, but it seems to help a lot of men.

In fact, it isn't long before it's broadcast to every sanctuary in the country. I get letters and emails about how much it's helped, and I continue to work hard on making it the most informative podcast it can be.

I call it *When Women Attack.*

EXCERPT FROM WHEN WOMEN ATTACKED PODCAST FINAL EPISODE (TRANSCRIPT)

It's an honour to have you with us today, Jason.

You are welcome.

I'll admit that I'm not a subscriber of your blog, but my sister used to be a big fan. I mean, a big, big fan – she obsessed over what you wrote. Barely an argument about feminism would pass without her bringing up your name.

I'm glad to hear this.

Firstly, of course, I have to ask you the question everyone probably asks. You are a male feminist. Do you ever get any stick for that?

(Chuckles.) Only from small-minded men. The kind of men who call themselves lads, and will claim I'm under the thumb or have smaller balls than them – which is metaphorical, I assume.

I would hope so.

It often amazes me how such people have the intelligence to use a metaphor.

It seems like you get quite irritated by lad culture.

You could say that. At least, the part of lad culture dominated by sexists. Those that believe that women were there to be shagged or stared at, back before they went feral – the kind that judged a woman's worth on how she presented herself. The kind that assumed a short skirt meant a woman wished to be harassed.

Some may be sceptical of your opinions, considering recent events.

I imagine so.

I mean, women have attacked men and wiped out a significant portion of the population. Our species is in danger. We live in constant fear. How can you be a woman sympathiser when such horrific acts are being committed by them?

It's simple, really. But if you ask that question you probably won't accept the answer.

I'm willing to be open-minded.

(Takes a moment.) I believe, Kevin, that what happened is not women's fault. It is men's.

Not women's fault?

Precisely.

You're losing me a bit here, I'm afraid, Jason. Surely it was women who attacked us? How are we responsible for that?

I thought you were willing to be open-minded.

Of course. Please, go on.

Okay. Well, let's really think about this. How long ago did this happen? How long is it since women turned on us?

It's going on thirty days now.

And how long has it been since men turned on women?

...I don't follow.

How long has the male patriarchy designed society's rules to favour them? How long has it been that marriage is the exchanging of the woman as property of the father to property of the husband? How long has it been that male patriarchy has told a woman she should be a housewife?

But such sexism has changed. More recently, I mean. We lived in a society where women can work, and when women are no longer owned by their husbands.

In the last, what, fifty years? Or, let's be generous – women got the vote about a hundred years ago. Let's say there's been more of a balance for a hundred years – even though there hasn't been, but for the sake of argument, let's just say there has.

Okay.

How significant is that hundred years compared to the thousands of years that preceded it? Our society has always – and I mean *always* – been designed to keep men in charge. Even most religions have been designed to suppress women. Notice how, in the ten commandments, it does not mention that one does not rape. It believes that not coveting what your neighbour has is more important.

Surely that's a sign of the times in which they were created.

Exactly! And although it is now understood that one does not rape, tell me – how many rapists are found guilty compared to how many are reported? And wasn't it only in 2003 that the illegality of marital rape was explicitly set out in the Sexual Offences Act – that's 2003, Kevin.

So this is about rape?

No, not at all. This is about far more discreet sexism than that.

I don't follow.

So if we accept that thousands of years of male patriarchy came to an end in the last fifty or so years – then we can assume that things are better now, right?

Yes, I guess so.

Then that assumption would be wrong, Kevin, as it means we completely disregard everyday sexism. I read books, and while the author writes that men shout, they write that women scream. I had a friend who's an actress, and she was consistently cast in two-dimensional roles as the love interest. A woman who is seen as moody is told to smile more. A woman is told they are being hysterical when a male colleague compliments their body and they say it's inappropriate, and that complaining about harassment is an overreaction. And the same men who make such derogatory remarks are always the same men who say it's okay as they would open the door for a woman, as if this excuses their behaviour.

I still don't understand how this links to recent events.

Because we are responsible for the way women have felt. In the end, we just pushed them too far.

But what about men like me? Men who don't catcall women, who don't treat women differently. Men who don't condescend or sexualise.

Ah, Kevin. What a brilliant question.

Well?

Men like you, if you are the kind of man you purport to be, are the ones who bring hope that this world can be restored to what it was – or, better yet, a world that is superior to what it was. Take your twin sister, Kaylee, for example.

Yes.

What happened?

She saved me.

Ah, see, that is where you are confused.

What?

You restored her faith. You showed her that a good man still exists, and that was crucial in her transformation.

I don't quite understand.

(Pauses.) You think she saved you, Kevin, but I am afraid you are mistaken. You see, in the end, it was the person you are that saved her.

I what?

And, so long as a man like you exists, we live in hope that we can restore the faith of womankind. That we can prove to women that it is worth returning to society as it was – albeit, with a little more balance.

You think that can happen?

Think? Kevin, I am sure of it.

Hm.

If we can prove ourselves worthy, hopefully we can welcome back womankind once again.

And if we can't?

If we can't? Well, then we are all doomed.

JOIN RICK WOOD'S READER'S GROUP FOR YOUR FREE BOOKS

Join at **www.rickwoodwriter.com/sign-up**

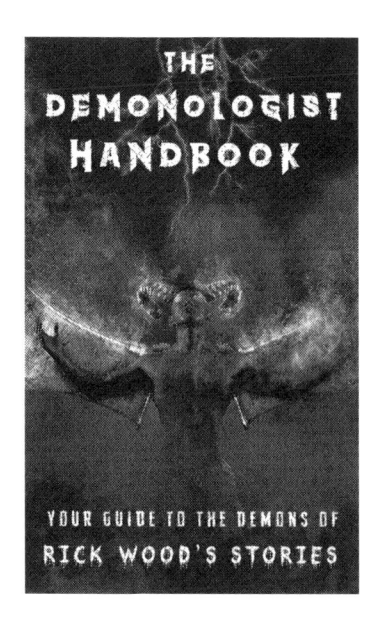

ALSO BY RICK WOOD...

RICK WOOD

THE SENSITIVES

THE SENSITIVES BOOK ONE

THIS BOOK IS FULL OF BODIES

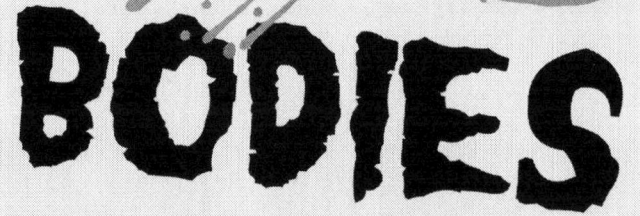

RICK WOOD

RICK WOOD

ROSES ARE RED SO IS YOUR BLOOD

RICK WOOD

SHUTTER HOUSE

Printed in Poland
by Amazon Fulfillment
Poland Sp. z o.o., Wrocław